NEW MOON RISING

/ / / /

J.R. RAIN
&
MATTHEW S. COX

SAMANTHA MOON ORIGINS

New Moon Rising
Pale Moon Calling
Dark Moon Falling

Published by
Crop Circle Books
212 Third Crater, Moon

Printed in the United States of America.

ISBN-13: 978-1977728111
ISBN-10: 1977728111

J.R. Rain:
To the wonderful fans. Love you all.

Matthew S. Cox:
Thank you for reading *New Moon Rising*! I'd also like to thank J.R. Rain for giving me the opportunity to work with him in the Samantha Moon world. This was an amazingly fun project and I am honored to have the opportunity to work with such a beloved character.

Chapter One
Three Seconds

July 2004

Optimistic that I'm going to finally enjoy a nice relaxing day, I settle into my folding beach chair and stretch my weary legs.

It's been almost a year of barely-controlled chaos with us closing on the house, moving, Danny and his buddy Jeff Rodriguez starting their own law firm, registering Tammy for preschool, child-proofing our new home so Anthony doesn't get into anything dangerous…ugh. When I first started working as an agent for the Department of Housing and Urban Development, I never imagined I'd think of going *to* work as a break.

But not today.

It's Saturday and for once, Danny's caseload is balanced enough that he can slip away. Over the past fifty some odd weekends, he's been away from the law firm maybe ten of them. Of course, that left me working on the house by myself while wrangling toddlers. I'm amazed he hasn't complained about such long hours, but he's got a much better chance of making the big bucks being the boss. Or one of the bosses. It is, however, a lot more work. With my relatively short tenure as a federal agent and his unpredictable income, taking on a mortgage has been... nail biting, to put it mildly.

Anyway, enough of that. We're here to unwind, at least for half a day. The sun's perched high in the cloudless sky, making the beach around us glow with heat blur. It's nice to finally be able to enjoy the warmth of catching a few rays. Back when I was attending Cal State Fullerton, I'd slip away to soak up the sun any chance I could get. Sadly, being able to do nothing on a Saturday hasn't happened in a while, and this body of mine isn't quite bikini ready. Oh, I mean I'm fit enough... the problem is, I think I'm blinding anyone who looks directly at me. Sorry, people.

Tammy's perched in a hole she's dug to my right, between our folding chairs, playing in the sand while Danny uses one hand to shield Anthony's eyes while spraying him with sunblock. Whoever invented aerosol sunscreen deserves the Nobel Prize. They were divinely inspired—or they, too, had tried to use cream-based sunblock on a two-year-old. Anthony fidgets and grunts in annoyance, but soon distracts himself by jabbing his little toy shovel at the sand.

"You're even prettier than the day we met." Danny leans over and kisses me. It's quick, since we *are* in public after all. Between his dark hair and deep, blue eyes, I could stare at him for hours. And kiss him for hours too. He sits on his beach chair and swings his legs up before lacing his fingers behind his head. "Coming out here today was the best idea you've had in weeks, babe. My eyes are vibrating from staring at documents."

I chuckle, watching Tammy work feverishly to expand her little den. "Don't even get me started with documents," I say. "Feels like all I do is stare at a computer."

He rolls his head to the right and smiles at me. "I sleep much better at night, you know that. If you'd gone FBI, I'd be a nervous wreck."

Anthony notices Tammy excavating, and decides the sand she's pushing up the sides of her hole ought to go back *in* the hole. He babbles urgently while shoveling it on top of her head.

"No! Anf-nee!" yells Tammy, whipping sand into the air as fast as she can move, spraying both Danny and me.

My son babbles at her while flicking dirt into her excavation. He thinks the beach is trying to 'eat' her and wants to help her. Judging by my husband's adoring grin, he's also learned to interpret two-year-old.

I stifle a laugh and hold up a finger to show Danny. "I got a paper cut Tuesday. Might have to pull desk duty until it heals." My implication is clear: work as a HUD agent isn't that exciting, although, in rare times, it can be.

As Tammy begins to reach critical meltdown mode, Danny grins and tugs Anthony back. Seconds before the explosion of screaming and tears starts, she sniffles at me as if to say, 'look what he did!' and resumes her quest to reach China.

Danny winks. "They should issue you protective gloves or something."

I lean back and close my eyes, basking in the warmth of the sun. It's wonderful to finally have a moment to relax where I don't *have* to do anything. Moments like this might be more common if I could ask my parents to watch the kids now and then, but they're still not really talking to me. Also, their little village might not be the best place for kids. Unless I'm *trying* to raise a pair of hippies. The locals up there might randomly walk around with lit bongs, or with nothing on. And that's not exactly a sight to appreciate. Their settlement is mostly old people who never quite got done with the sixties, weed, and free love. And, well, my taking a job for the government didn't sit well with my parents. They don't want my 'mind control vibes' around their sanctuary. I tried to explain what I really do, but Mom and Dad are both convinced I've 'turned evil' or been brainwashed by The Man.

Oh well. Their loss. Not like they ever really got involved in my life beyond creating me. My older sister Mary Lou basically looked out for me when we were kids. She's six years older with a strong nurturing instinct. Between my brothers and me, she never needed dolls.

Right. Beach. Sun. Day off. Not time to dwell on my crazy parents.

Tammy lets out a shriek like a miniature Xena. I open my eyes and start to sit upright as she springs at Anthony and whacks him upside the head with her little fist. He reacts by staring in total confusion. Tammy stomps her foot, points at the hole she's been trying to dig, and yells, "No!"

Anthony looks at her, blinks, and prattles. "No eee bee Tammy."

I think he's saying he doesn't want the beach to eat her. She draws her fist back to pop him again, but Danny grabs the boy and whisks him up into his arms.

"Be right back." He nods toward a distant Italian ice vendor. "Time for my old standby negotiating tactic."

"Bribery?" I wink.

He rolls his eyes. "Peace offerings aren't bribery. A gift with *hope* of something happening is not the same as a gift with the *requirement* of something happening."

"Right." I grin at my attorney hubby before giving Tammy the stern face and tugging her close. "We've talked about hitting, haven't we?"

She flails her arms. "But Mom! I asked him'a stop 'frowing sand on me, but he keep 'frowing sand on my hair. He wouldn't listen!"

"I know, sweetie." I brush sand out of her hair.

"But hitting is the wrong way to handle a problem. What *should* you have done?"

"Sued him?" Tammy tilts her head.

It's difficult to stay upset when exposed to that much cute. I can't help but laugh. The child grins, knowing she got me.

"Where did you hear that from?" I ask.

"Daaaadddy." Tammy digs her toes into the sand.

Of course. Oh, please don't let her grow up to be an ambulance chaser. "Well, sweetie. Suing people is—"

Her gaze shifts to the left, looking past me the exact moment the sudden feeling of being watched falls on my shoulders like ice water. My heart slams in my chest. For an instant, I feel like I'm the girl in the horror movie with the monster behind her she doesn't see. But hey, I'm a brunette. The dark-haired one usually survives.

I whip around, one hand going for my purse (and duty weapon), but freeze at finding empty sand. The most menacing thing anywhere near me is a borderline-obese seagull with its head stuck in an empty French fry carton. Still, the sensation like I'm about to be sliced open by a serial killer hasn't weakened. Despite my staring into open air, my skin crawls like I've come eye-to-eye with true evil.

Beachgoers fade into the periphery of my awareness; the rush of my breathing roars as loud as Niagara Falls. In the middle of a sweltering beach, I shiver, my arms prickling with goosebumps. Any second now, I know I'm going to die.

What the hell is happening?

Heaviness presses in on my chest, robbing the breath from my lungs and making each heartbeat painful. I reach to my right and back, searching for Tammy, trying to put myself between whatever *this* is and my child. The instant my fingers make contact with her shoulder, all the dread vanishes.

"The woman's gone, Mommy," says Tammy in an eerie calm tone.

I blink, gazing mesmerized at the empty beach for a second more before whipping my head around to stare at her. "What? What woman?"

"The one who was watching you." Tammy points at a spot of open sand about ten feet away. "She's not there anymore."

I stare at the conspicuous lack of footprints, but can't argue that the foreboding evil had seemed to be coming from that exact place. After snagging my purse, I stand, stuffing my hand inside to grab my sidearm, but not drawing it. Out of the corner of my eye, I note Danny and Anthony about two hundred yards off at the ice vendor, in line. No one nearby is acting odd… well, no one except for me.

After creeping a few steps forward, I crouch to examine the ground, but the undisturbed sand proves no one had been there. Ugh. Maybe the stress really is getting to me? How messed up is it that taking a day to escape stress winds up causing it? But, my kid saw someone. I twist back to face her. "What did this wom—?"

Tammy's gone.

Alarm bells go off in my head. I spin about in a circle, searching, but don't see any purple. She's in a purple swimsuit with a little skirt frill and pink flip-flops. At the realization my brain is framing up her description for a police report, my panic turns everything around me to a blur of color and meaningless sound.

"Tammy?" I call, not quite screaming, on my way back to the hole she dug. Her flops are still beside it, like someone grabbed her and plucked her straight out of them. "Tammy!" I shout, turning.

A few people look at me.

No! This isn't happening.

"Holy shit!" yells a man.

I stare at him and he dives to the beach from his chair. Oh, crap. My gun's out. "Calm down. I'm a federal agent." Back in the purse it goes. "Have you seen my daughter? She's four? Purple bathing suit, black hair?"

He (and the woman sitting beside him) shake their heads, still staring at me like I'm a psycho.

"Tammy?" I call again, spinning in place.

Anthony and Danny are still at the ice vendor, not having noticed me shouting. Really? All it takes is looking away for three seconds and a child can vanish. I know this, but seriously?! Not Tammy! Not my daughter! Come on, Sam, think! I force fear and panic into a box and slam the lid down on their arms. Shaking with nerves, I try to assess my surroundings. Nothing in our 'campsite' is disturbed, nor are any adult-sized footprints obvious, other than the trail Danny left.

I don't see anyone hurrying off with a small child in tow, no signs of a disturbance in the crowd, and most alarmingly, no screaming Tammy calling for her mother. A line of small depressions in the sand *could* be her footprints leading off. I follow the trail up the beach for about sixty feet, heading away from the water, but it's soon indistinguishable when the tracks merge with an area of heavy foot traffic.

People jostle around me on both sides, their arms laden with folding chairs, umbrellas, coolers, and portable stereos. What's wrong with them all? They don't care that my child is missing? Why are they going on about their business like the Earth hasn't just stopped rotating? One guy bumps me a little hard with his giant blue Coleman cooler, then has the nerve to glare at me.

With a snarl, I give him a shove that knocks him over sideways, and trot a few steps farther in the same direction the footprints led me. I spin, searching in a circle, but there are no four-year-olds in purple swimsuits anywhere in sight.

"Tammy!" I scream, getting a few looks.

Shit!

I yank my cell phone from my purse and open the contacts list, hunting for Denise Pagano, an FBI agent who I wound up assisting my second month on the job. We became fast friends, and I'm not above calling in a favor for something like this.

My head swims with lectures about the first

forty-eight hours being the most critical when children are abducted. Stranger abductions are rarer than people think—but they're also the most dangerous for the child. Tears stream down my cheeks. I know all the stats and timelines, but it's not supposed to happen to *my* daughter!

Two seconds after I press the cell phone against my ear, my undirected gaze lands on a skinny little girl in a purple swimsuit, thirty feet away by a row of booths and stands near the parking area. It's Tammy! She sways side to side, grinning up at an older gray-haired man with a large belly, white T-shirt, and blue Bermuda shorts. He's smiling, but looking around more than at her. My stomach starts to clench, but I get the sense he's wondering where her parents are, not hoping to evade being seen.

I sprint across the parking area, heading straight for them. The old man looks at me and points at Tammy as if to ask, 'is she yours?' My nerves calm ever so slightly when he reacts to my nod with a relieved slouch.

Tammy's in the midst of telling this man about her favorite show, *Barney & Friends*. I heard a rumor that the CIA was considering using long-term exposure to it as an interrogation technique, but I'd gladly have it on 24/7 in exchange for never being this worried ever again. After vaulting a row of plain, backless benches between the storefronts and the lot, I swoop in on my kid.

She squeals with delight when I haul her into the air and squeeze her close. "Tammy! You scared me to death!"

"It's all right, miss," says the old man. "Your little sister's fine."

I lift my face from the crook of Tammy's neck to peer quizzically at the guy. Either his eyes are shot or he's giving me a compliment. "Little sister? Oh, thanks. She's my daughter."

He raises two bushy white eyebrows. "Pardon me. You look young." He chuckles. "Guess everyone looks young when you're my age."

"Sorry, Mommy. Mr. Feagans looked lonely."

The man waves to Tammy before tipping his fisherman's cap at me. "Beautiful daughter you've got there. Speaking of beautiful, I'd best get on back to my wife."

I nod at him, unable to decide if I should thank him for watching her or be upset that his evident loneliness attracted her.

"Sam?" Danny jogs up to me, masterfully balancing Anthony in one arm and three Italian ices in the other hand. "What's up? Why are you all the way over here?"

I lean against him, still clinging to Tammy. She gets squirmy with the treats in sight, so I shift enough to let her grab one, and she goes right for the blue ice. "Looked away for a couple seconds, and she disappeared."

Danny's expression darkens. Before he can ask me how I can 'just lose her like that,' I explain that weird feeling I got, like someone was sneaking up behind me with a knife.

"She didn't have a knife, Mommy." Tammy shakes her head.

"You saw this woman too?" Danny blinks at her.

Tammy bites her ice, making both Danny and me cringe. "Yeah."

"Please, don't you *ever* run off like that again, okay?" I hug her tight.

Danny offers me one of the two remaining cherry ices, his expression softening. "You okay, hon?"

All the air in my lungs blasts out in a heavy sigh. "Yeah. I swear... our daughter is too nice. She'd trust the Devil himself if he said hello."

A sly grin spreads over my husband's face. "I can ask Mr. Westfield over for dinner if you want to test that."

If there's anyone in this world I'd gladly go to my grave without ever seeing again, it's Danny's former boss at the old law firm. "Let's not." Ooh. The ice has actual bits of cherry in it. "I'm going to need another weekend at the beach to recover from our weekend at the beach," I say.

Danny laughs, and we head back to our spot. As much as I try to enjoy the rest of the day, I'm unable to pull my eyes off Tammy and Anthony. I have no explanation for what happened. Tammy saw someone watching me, yet nothing had been there. My parents are all into that spiritualistic crap, and up until a few minutes ago, if anyone had asked me if I believed such a thing as true evil exists—not just 'politicians screwing over the little guy' evil—I'd have said no.

Now, I'm not so sure.

Chapter Two
A Little Work

No weekend in the present life of Samantha Moon would be complete without a whole bunch of work. At least the rest of Saturday was relaxing. Sunday morning post-breakfast is a blur. Danny ran off soon after a call from Jeff Rodriguez about a case they're working on. Evidently, a serious amount of money's at stake, and he needed to meet with the client *today*.

Damn.

I can't complain too much. We need Danny to get paid. Maybe we jumped on the whole house thing a little earlier than prudent, but our old apartment was too small. Tammy had the second bedroom, really a glorified closet, and Anthony's crib shared our room. We couldn't put him in Tammy's room, and no boy wants to grow up sharing a bedroom with his parents. Soon after

Danny and Jeff opened their own practice, the naïve belief that he'd essentially won the lotto carried us into a realtor's place.

Only, that firehose of money never materialized. I'm not doing *too* bad pay wise; it's steady at least. Granted, my income is presently more than Danny's, which has made for more than a few episodes of Moody Hubby. He's got the potential to make a lot more, but it's not easy to bootstrap a new law firm up from zero. They've poached a few clients that he used to work with from his former firm, and I think he's had a few referrals from his buddy Mike at the auto body place.

So, yeah. We're hanging onto the dream, even if we are one unexpected financial crisis away from complete disaster.

Anyway, we managed to swing a pretty good deal on the house. Despite having been a 'fixer-upper,' all that backbreaking work is finished a bit over a year after moving in. No one looking at it now would ever be able to guess what the place looked like when we closed. Our single-story home is in a hilly area above Harbor Boulevard. It's nicely larger than we expected to reach with our budget as well, and a stone's throw from Hillcrest Park. Four bedrooms worked out perfectly. One each for the kids, a master, and another one that's become my 'office' because it has a sliding glass door. Except for the office, the rest of the rooms are on the tiny side. When we redid the floors, we went for hardwood in the halls and carpet in the rooms, and nice black and white tile floors for the bathrooms. We poured a lot of effort into the place, and it's become home.

In fact, the only part of this house that I'm not absolutely thrilled with is the detached garage.

It irks me because it happens to contain our washer and dryer, meaning I have to go outside and get rained on to do laundry—just like our days in an apartment when I had to drive to the laundromat. Only now, we had to pay for the machines as well. Fortunately, the day's clear, and I suppose walking twenty feet still beats a ten-minute car ride. Maybe when money isn't such a problem, we can have some contractors come in and build a laundry room or something.

Tammy and Anthony zip around our front yard, which is fortunately enclosed in chain link fence. Mary Lou suggested a fun idea for the kids to do next holiday: run colored streamers through the links. Maybe that'll become our tradition or something. After yesterday at the beach, I barely take my eyes off them while lugging a giant basket of dirty laundry over to the open garage.

My battered pale blue 'momvan' sits in the driveway, offset a bit so Danny's BMW can get in too. He picked it up used. Despite having like three hundred thousand miles on it, the body and interior are in great shape so it 'looks the part' for his law career. He could've gotten a new Chevy or Ford for what he's paying on that old Beemer, but he thinks rolling up in a 'Joe Everyman' car will make people think he's a bad lawyer.

I call the kids over to keep them in sight while I load the washing machine. By some miracle, they both come running without protest, though Anthony trips over the side of the driveway and takes a pratfall. He's got three speeds: standing still, running, and sliding on his face. He shakes it off, giggling, and scrambles in behind his sister, who begins exploring the forest of cardboard boxes filling the garage.

This weekend is the first one since we moved in where we are officially done with renovating. No painting, tiling, patching drywall, installing new sinks, moving crap around, or anything else hanging over us—hence, the beach. Nothing like a few hours absorbing sunlight to melt away stress. Except, what happened yesterday added a whole bunch more.

Once I've got the laundry in and the machine running, I walk the kids around to the backyard and set them loose on the sandbox Danny made them. My outdoor lounge chair might be from Walmart, but it's comfortable. With the kids in view, the whirr of the washing machine in my left ear, and my butt sinking into the (okay, I admit it's hideous) green and white cushion, I get about as close to perfect as I think possible.

The future's looking pretty bright, and I'm already wearing shades. We still have a lot of work ahead of us, but the drudgery is behind. Our little place in Fullerton is hardly paradise, but it finally feels like I've got a handle on this whole 'life' thing.

A grin spreads across my face while I watch my kids building a sandcastle together. For so long, I've had this nagging doubt that I scraped by on the help of others. It might've taken me 'til thirty-one to stretch my wings and feel like a real functioning adult, but I'm finally doing it.

Chapter Three
Pushing Paper

Some people think that humanity faces darkness in two inevitable forms: death and taxes. There's a third inevitable darkness: Mondays.

I often wonder while staring at screen after screen of mind-numbing charts and data if we were better off before the bulk of the population wound up having to work wage jobs to survive. Maybe we had it better living in the days before the nine-to-five, when we hunter/gatherers roamed the plains or people lived in tiny villages with self-sufficient farms and neighbors who not only actually spoke with each other, but knew the names of distant relatives... because they lived just down the road.

On the other hand, they also had short life expectancies and generally wallowed in filth, so maybe a boring office job isn't so bad after all. It might've been slow and relaxing to live like that, but winding up dead because you accidentally nicked your finger while cutting food… yeah, screw that.

A flurry of rapid-fire keystrokes announce my partner, Chad Helling, has either been drawn into an email argument with his girlfriend or he's taking a routine report way too far. His desk occupies a cube across from mine, amid a sea of almost-eye-level gray fabric walls. The rug between us has this mesmerizing pattern of little squares that will suck the soul straight out of anyone who stares into it too long. Maybe the carpet is part of the brainwashing my parents are so convinced the government uses.

Before starting here, I expected it to be like those police procedurals from TV where agents and their partners have desks facing each other, in a room full of other agents whose desks face each other, and lots of shouting, cursing, and crude humor. The HUD field office is almost indistinguishable from any typical cube farm, except for the federal logos on the walls and the blackout filters on our computer screens to prevent casual eavesdropping.

Speaking of close to the monitor, I force daydreams of living in a cottage off in the woods somewhere out of my head and get back to the task at hand: routine audits of randomly selected people who are receiving housing assistance. After maybe an hour of that, my cubicle wall creaks.

"You look like you could use some more coffee," says Chad.

He's a couple years younger than me, taller, short brown hair in a military brush cut. The man's athletic and muscular, but always wears loose button-down white shirts that conceal his shape. I only know what he really looks like because he insisted I go to one of his amateur MMA fights. He didn't have a shirt on for that, and those boxer shorts showed off quite a bit of his legs too. Chad's no Hercules, but if I'd never met Danny, some sparks might've flown between us. As nice as he may be to admire from a distance, he doesn't hold a candle to the love of my life. Danny might not be able to kick a man ten feet across a ring or lift—well, however much weight Chad can lift—but he's sweet, caring, intelligent, devoted… and yeah, he's cute too.

I stop smiling at Danny's picture to the right of my screen and glance up at my partner. "Yeah. I don't think there's enough coffee in the world."

"Rough weekend?" Chad holds up his mug in a 'come on, let's go' way.

"Just a few minutes of heart-stopping terror. Otherwise, it was pretty relaxing." My mug dangling from a finger, I follow him down the walkway between cubes to the break room at the end of the row.

"Oh, I gotta hear this," says Chad.

On the way to the coffee machine and while we pour, I explain Tammy's disappearing.

Chad chuckles while dumping creamer powder in and stirring. "Kids… Glad it wound up being innocent. Makes the boredom a little nicer."

"Yeah. I'd much rather be bored here than racing in circles on a beach looking for my missing daughter. Though, it's been extra boring lately. Feels like I'm in *Office Space*, only with a gun on my hip."

Chad laughs. "Not exactly the 007 life you were dreaming about in the academy?"

"Hardly." I take a sip of java—black—which makes him wince. "At least we're doing something good here, right?"

He starts for the door. "If you say so."

"There's honest people who need help getting by, and not-so-honest people stealing that help."

Chad stops and leans on the entrance to his cube, slurps coffee, and flares his eyebrows. "You make HUD sound glorious. We're armed accountants."

I smirk. "Tell that to Arturo Rosales."

He cringes. "Okay, fair point... but the DEA doesn't borrow us that often."

Speaking of borrow. I need to return Denise's voicemail asking why I called. The FBI sometimes grabs HUD agents for extra bodies, usually on warrant raids or for search parties. A month on the job, and my butt was tromping around the woods helping hunt for a missing twelve-year-old girl who'd disappeared with her non-custodial father. They'd wound up in our territory all the way from Maine. Sometimes, those cases aren't so nerve-wracking, but this guy was one of those batshit crazy anti-government gun wonks, and we all thought he'd shoot his daughter and off himself before letting the wife have her back. It had a somewhat-happy ending. The kid had the hell scared out of her, but she's okay physically. Her dad wasn't so lucky. We'd all gone in plainclothes, pretending to be 'lost hikers,' since this guy would've freaked if he saw FBI logos or any kind of uniformed agent. The team who found the cabin and made contact spooked him somehow, and he went for a weapon. It didn't end well for him.

Anyway, back to my computer.

Hours melt away in an unending cascade of forms. Some of these people's handwriting is so damn awful I wonder how on Earth they made it out of school. When I hit one where a guy filled out his application with an orange crayon, I'm not sure if I should laugh or feel bad for the man. It's either a prank or mental issues.

"Hey," says Chad. "Hungry? It's like one already."

"Damn, is it? I'm having so much fun I thought it was almost five."

He sputters. "I wish. Ready for lunch?"

"Yeah. Need at least an hour of sun or these fluorescents will sap all my vitamins." I heard that once on Oprah. And I always believe Oprah.

We head out past the security desk and hop in our plain gray government-issue sedan HUD inherited from the FBI a year or two ago. The patched bullet hole in the headrest behind me isn't what one would call a 'confidence booster,' but as far as I know, the agent had been taking cover behind the door at the time. As new agents, we got last pick from motor pool, but it doesn't bother me the car's seen better days. My momvan's about the same, only with about a third the miles as this poor car (and no bullet holes). Shiny and new doesn't matter to me—that's Danny's thing. I prefer stuff that works, appearance be damned.

A couple blocks from the field office, we stop at this sushi place Chad likes. It helps that they run a lunch special menu, which makes it a frequent destination. Raw fish isn't really my scene, but I suppose anyone living in California these days has to at least be able to tolerate it in small doses if they ever want to go out with friends. Fortunately, they've got hot food as well.

After ordering my usual *nabeyaki udon* lunch, (basically chicken noodle soup with some extra bells and whistles—the egg floating in it is probably why I love it so much) I call Mary Lou. The phone rings for a while and dumps to voicemail. Huh? That's odd… She's watching the kids, so she should have her phone close by. Hmm. Maybe she's in the bathroom.

Chad and I gripe about the endless sea of paperwork, and this slimeball, Curtis Price—our first major success. He'd applied for and gotten fully-subsidized HUD housing under a false name while claiming to be a disabled veteran. In reality, the man earned close to a million a year as a music promoter, and used the house as a place to 'entertain' his artists. He's still living rent-free off the government, but his room's *much* smaller now.

I dial Mary Lou again, and Ellie Mae, her six-year-old, answers. She's given all her kids 'double names' like hers. Ellie's the eldest. She whispers, "Hi Aunt Sam."

What's with the whispering? Kids do weird things sometimes. "Hey, sweetie. Are you guys having fun?"

"No." Ellie Mae sounds sad and frightened. "Mommy's making us hide 'cause someone bad's outside."

I blink. "What? Someone bad? Are you okay?"

Chad stops chewing and stares at me. "That doesn't sound good."

My 'yeah, I know' stare makes him put his chopsticks down and lean closer to listen. "What's your mom doing right now?"

"She's on the 911," whispers Ellie Mae. "We're s'posed ta be quiet."

Anthony's babbling starts up in the background with Tammy and Billy Joe (my sister's four-year-old son) shushing him.

"What did you see?" I ask.

"Mommy told us to hide in here and be quiet," whispers Ellie Mae.

The squeak of a door comes over the line, then the rustle of a cell phone being handed off.

"Sam?" asks my sister, her voice quivering.

"I'm here, Mary Lou. I can be there in five

minutes. What's going on?"

She breathes into the phone for a few seconds like she's trying to calm down. "I thought there was someone prowling around the house. They're gone now. I called the police, and they're sending a car by to check."

"They won't find anything," says Tammy in the background.

My heart races.

"What?" asks Mary Lou.

I can just picture Tammy giving my sister the creepy-calm stare. "That bad lady doesn't make footprints."

"Uhh." Mary Lou sounds like she's on the verge of a panic attack.

"Mary... can you let me talk to Tammy for a sec?"

The phone changes hands without a word.

"Hi, Mommy," chirps Tammy.

Chad tilts his head, a look of concern in his eyes. "You okay? You're going pale."

"Yeah, it's nothing," I mutter to him while covering the phone. "Tam... did you see that same woman?"

"Yes, Mommy. But it's okay. She made a face at Aunt Mary Lou like you smellin' what Daddy did in the bathroom, an' went away."

I'm not sure if I should laugh or commit myself to a full-on panic attack. This doesn't make any sense at all. "Okay, sweetie. I'll see you in a couple hours, 'kay?"

"Okay," she chimes. "I love you, Mommy."

"Love you too, Tam Tam."

"Say hi to Mommy," mumbles Tammy.

Distorted babbling tells me Anthony's chewing on the cell phone while attempting to speak. Mary Lou takes the phone back and asks in a shaky voice, "What was she talking about? What woman?"

"Umm." I'd dismiss it as a kid thing, but my daughter's imaginary friend shouldn't have made me feel like death itself stared at me. I run through a quick explanation of the black shape she described from the beach. My daughter couldn't tell me if the woman was old or young, or even what her face looked like, more a silhouette of wispy darkness with a human shape and piercing white eyes. How that kid isn't having nightmares, I have no idea. Where did she get that image from? Of course, she made it up. Right?

"Oh." Mary Lou laughs off her fear. "I probably saw some of the neighborhood teens cutting across yards. I don't know why it spooked me so much."

Chad waves his hand around in a small circular motion, trying to pull more details out of me.

"You sure you're okay?" I ask.

"Fine." Mary Lou lets out a long breath. "Oh, the police are here. I gotta go."

"All right. Call me if anything else happens, okay?"

"Sure, Sam. Hey, I'm the one who should be worried about *you* getting hurt."

"I'll be extra careful. This file I'm working on

has a bad attitude. I think it's planning to cut me." I chuckle to myself, but my sister's right. Sometimes I do wind up in dangerous situations. People abusing the HUD program can get violent when we show up, which is the reason we pack heat.

"Bye." Mary Lou hangs up.

"So, what was that all about?" asks Chad.

"My sister thought she saw someone trying to break into her house, but she's always been overly cautious."

Chad, looking at me, adds too much of that green stuff to his next piece of sushi and makes a wild face when he eats it. His cough blasts the smell of horseradish into the air. "Oof. Little too much wasabi there."

"Even our food is trying to kill us." I raise one eyebrow at him.

Laughing makes him choke more. He dabs his mouth with a napkin and wipes a tear from his eye. "She's right to be vigilant. Woman home alone with kids? It's either nothing or an opportunistic burglar who panicked and ran off when he noticed someone there."

"Yeah," I say, not meaning it. Tammy describing some shadowy thing has me on edge, and inexplicable, crippling fear hand-in-hand with my kid seeing a shadow figure isn't the sort of topic one can openly discuss around federal agents without risking an appointment with a psychiatrist.

Chad holds up his chopsticks, a piece of ginger pinched between them. "Don't worry. If some guy meant to hurt her, he'd have broken in long before the cops got there."

I stare across the table at him, my expression flat. "Thanks. That's reassuring."

"That's why I'm here." He winks and eats the ginger.

Maybe I shouldn't worry just yet. Mary Lou and her family have lived in that place for years without anything happening. It's weird that two days after that thing shows up on the beach, it's at my sister's house, too. Wait. What? *That thing*? I'm really thinking about this like some actual ghost or whatever is stalking… Tammy? She's the only common link. I fidget in the chair, barely able to keep from leaping to my feet and rushing off to make sure she's all right. But, Tammy didn't seem the least bit afraid of it.

Stop. I rub my forehead, trying to force sanity through my skull. There's nothing phantasmal stalking my daughter, or me, or my sister. I must've reached some critical point of boredom at work that my brain has kicked into overdrive and I'm making shit up.

"You okay?" asks Chad, sounding sincere. "The police are there, and I'm sure it's nothing. We can swing by if you want. Say we were doing a property inspection."

"And then we'd have to falsify a report about a property we didn't really inspect." I sigh. "Nah, it's fine."

He grins. "Not if we really stopped by a place.

These inspections don't have time parameters."

"No, really. It's okay." I manage a smile.

A playful argument about paying starts when the check arrives. Our usual routine is to alternate, but he's 'forgotten' who's turn it is, and points out his $22 lunch was more expensive than my $13 soup. I relent this time, but make it clear tomorrow's on me.

We're not back in the office two minutes when Nico Fortunato, our boss, leans out of his door at the end of the row and gives us the 'get in here now' wave.

Uh oh.

Chapter Four
Idle Hands

"Well…" I glance across the aisle at Chad, who hadn't even made it all the way into his cube. "At least he doesn't look pissed."

With a 'yeah, good point' shrug, he falls in step behind me. Before we can get to his office, Nico hurries out and off to the left, waving for us to follow. He ducks into one of the medium-sized conference rooms where another six agents seated around a table all look up at us simultaneously. Though none fire off accusing stares, I feel like we've delayed the party taking a late lunch. Without a word, Chad and I settle into open seats near the door.

"All right, everyone." Nico approaches a dry erase board at the front end of the room. "We will be assisting in an operation involving FBI and ICE in about an hour. They are moving in on Juan Manuel Villero." He clicks a remote and an overhead projector on the ceiling puts the image of a thirtyish man with deep brown skin on the blank white wall. "He's a prominent figure in the local narcotics scene. According to the FBI, he has links to numerous gangs in our area as well as in Mexico. They've been tracking shipments of cocaine, heroin, and meth originating from Tijuana and Mexicali, which we believe Villero is acting as a distribution hub for, then sending the cash back up the line."

Murmurs and nods go around the room.

Chad taps me on the arm with the back of his hand and mutters, "Here's that boredom buster you were asking for."

Nico points to the projected face of a man who looks like any other guy next door, hardly a murderous criminal... but then again, all the most successful ones are adept at blending in. "The FBI intercepted a runner with close to three hundred grand heading back to the supplier in Mexico. We expect this has, or soon will, cause pressure for Mr. Villero. We need to close the net before he disappears."

I stare at the man on the wall, my mind racing back to my training running the tactical course. This will be only the third time I've gone into a 'live fire' situation. We help other agencies out here and there, so it's not *too* unusual. That they're pulling in so many extra people gets me a little worried. Drug gangs like this—especially with that much money floating around—usually have hardware like M-16s or AK47s. Hopefully, whoever's running this bust is hoping an overwhelming federal presence will intimidate the thugs into surrendering without violence, and he's not just adding every agent he can find to the raid because he's expecting a firefight from hell.

Nico clicks the remote again and the image changes to a smallish house surrounded by scrub brush and dirt. A single beat-up Nissan sits beside the house, its 'driveway' little more than a strip of dirt. "This is the property Juan Manuel Villero is using as his operations center. In case any of you are wondering why we are involved, it's a HUD home."

A few agents sigh with a 'that figures' resignation. Chad shakes his head. Every time one of these scumballs takes a house away from a needy, honest family, we both get pissed. I lean forward, studying the yellowish-brown building.

"The property is registered to a woman by the name of Rosa María Melendez. What her relationship is with Mr. Villero is undetermined." Nico hands out a stack of papers to everyone. "Miss Melendez secured the property three years ago, before Villero was on the FBI's radar. We don't know whether she obtained the house for him or if he found her after the fact. That'll be our issue to sort out once the dust settles and the DEA's vacuuming up all the coke."

Agent Ernie Montoya laughs.

"Bet she's not reporting that income," says Chad with a wink.

Chuckles go around the room.

Nods and murmurs of agreement rise from the agents. I flip open the document packet and study more photos of the home, the HUD application, a copy of Rosa's driver's license, and a few aerial photographs showing a fenced-in backyard with a short stretch of dirt and trees between it and another road. Those photos show a white van parked by the Nissan.

"Any questions?" asks Nico.

"What's our role going to be here?" asks Bryce Anders. He's been with HUD six years, and is our resident by-the-book type.

Nico nods at him. "Your initial role during the raid will be containment. The FBI/DEA/ICE team will be knocking"—that's 'Nico-speak' for kicking the door down—"our team will be providing additional perimeter coverage."

Bryce fidgets. He's been wanting to transfer to the FBI or DEA, so this has got to be exciting for him. Hearing that we'll pretty much be in the back watching for runners disappoints him.

"Anything else?" Nico rocks back on his heels, silver eyebrows up.

Michelle Rivera holds up her packet. "What kind of hardware are these guys throwing around?"

"The eyes we have on the property haven't reported a significant display of weapons, but with the amount of money involved here, we are operating under the assumption they are well armed." Nico looks around at us. "You'll all have

M4s and tactical vests."

Crap. I've barely used the M4. Only on the range for the mandatory evaluations.

"Anyone have a psych work up on this guy?" asks Montoya. Ernie's the most senior of our group, and the agent I spent my first month shadowing. "Is this guy going to freak out and try to take as many of us with him as possible, or likely to surrender?"

Nico sets his hands on his hips and sighs. "The FBI, if they have that information, didn't share. I think they got lucky and tripped over this guy. He's a US citizen, born in Amarillo. His record's got a couple of minor arrests in his early twenties, but nothing violent. We know he's got at least one relative in Mexicali, a first cousin. The FBI believes he's the contact on the other side."

"If Villero's a citizen, what's ICE doing here?" asks Michelle. "They can't revoke citizenship if he was born in Texas."

"No, but they believe his associates are in the country illegally," says Nico.

Montoya shuffles his papers. "How many suspects in the residence?"

"You'll be coordinating with FBI Special Agent Will Martin. He'll be able to provide a more accurate idea, but from what I've seen, I'd expect four to six."

On any other day, I'd be nervous—who wouldn't be—but after the beach? I have no explanation for that, but I can't remember ever being so paralyzed with fear before in my life. Not talking about when Tammy vanished, I mean that sense of something predatory hovering around me. At least, I haven't been that terrified since I'd been about five. One night, my parents' crystal skull bong caught the moonlight and glowed on the windowsill. (At the time, we all shared one giant bedroom.) I thought it was a demon or something and screamed my head off.

I once read this article about the difference between fear and terror. It described *fear* as the way you feel if you're trapped in a car with a huge dog on the hood growling at you, ready to rip you to shreds if you open the door. Terror happens when that dog's eyes start glowing red.

Well, that damn dog's eyes lit up bright on the beach last Saturday.

After feeling that, the idea of raiding a drug den doesn't bother me as much as it should. At least, no worse than the second or two of consideration that any time I get in a car, I could wind up dead. Nico dismisses us after no one comes up with any more questions. Once back at my cube, I pull up the records we have for the property.

Rosa Melendez, the property owner, applied for HUD assistance as single, no dependents. She's a twenty-eight-year-old lawful permanent resident with a 'green card.' Looks like she applied for naturalization, but they denied her due to her not being in the country for five years yet. No criminal record, and according to the file, she works for Universal Maintenance Services, a company that does contract cleaning for corporate offices. That beat-up twelve-year-old Nissan is registered in her name. Twentyish minutes of digging up tax returns and bank statements later, I'm convinced she doesn't have any unreported income streams... unless she's stuffing cash in her mattress.

"Hmm. Rosa looks clean."

Chad rolls his chair back enough to look at me past the cube wall. "What?"

"Been checking up on the Melendez woman. Nothing's out of place."

"She might have other bank accounts under false names."

I shrug at him. "Either that or she doesn't have a whole lot of choice about what's going on in her house."

Chad's eyebrows tilt up. "Nervous? I thought you were bored. It'll be nice to get out of the office again... you know they love to borrow us because 'HUD agents have nothing else to do.'"

"Ha!" I chuckle. "Not really nervous... more hoping if this woman's as innocent as she appears to be, she doesn't wind up catching a bullet."

"Yeah." Chad looks down. "Maybe we'll luck out and these guys will see an army of feds and shit their pants."

I glance sideways at the clock. Time to go. "Here's hoping. Ready?"

"Yeah. You?"

"As ready as I guess I can be." I lock the computer and grab my gear.

Chapter Five
Field Trip

I wind up driving this time, following a pair of black Chevy Suburbans and another 'inconspicuous' sedan like ours.

Chad fidgets at the straps holding his tactical vest on. Yes, it feels strange, rigid and tight, but I'm *not* one of those agents who bitches about having to put body armor on. Hell, I'm more uncomfortable at having my hair up. Nico's fine with me leaving it down at the office, but it'll only get in the way on a raid. Small price to pay.

Normally, they give us lighter bulletproof vests that we can wear under our clothes, but these are blue versions of what combat infantrymen wear. Heavy duty shit that can supposedly stop an assault rifle round. Maybe it's less bothersome to me since I'm on the slender side. It sure seems to be bugging my partner.

Danny's like that a bit with dress shirts. He loathes tight collars, the way they squeeze and rub his neck. His grandmother had a thing about 'how boys should dress,' so whenever they visited, he got stuck in a button-down and slacks. Kinda weird for a lawyer to hate dressy clothes, but at least he's not stuck with the strangulation shirts (as he called them) his mother used to make him wear.

The blasé feeling I'd had toward this raid while in the office chips away with each passing mile. I can't explain it, but some inner sense whispers at me that something's not right. Chad has his game face on, as usual, while my knuckles whiten on the wheel. This is a new feeling, though I'm quite certain I'm not psychic. What am I saying? Psychics? That's no more real than witchcraft. No... I'm letting my imagination run away with itself after that nonsense on the beach.

And at my sister's house.

Deep breath in. Deep breath out.

Our caravan pulls off the expressway, headed for the outskirts of Palmdale. The area around Rosa's house is pretty wide open, so the FBI has set up a rally point a few blocks away out of sight. After parking, we all gather up in the shadow of a huge, blue transport truck. Two men in black BDUs and bulletproof vests with yellow FBI markings hand us each a Colt M4 from a weapons rack in the truck, plus a nylon belt with two extra 30-round magazines.

Holy crap... what exactly are they expecting

here?

I check my weapon, ensuring it's got a round chambered and is on safe. We all had to go through range time with them, but this is the first time I've had one in the field for real. When we helped Denise comb the forest for that abducted girl, our standard sidearms had been plenty.

Chad takes his carbine and checks it over. In his hands, it looks small, almost like it wants to be an assault rifle when it grows up. For me, it's about perfect. Well, as perfect as a killing machine can get. He slings it over his shoulder on the strap and walks across the street to where a striking man with short black hair and piercing blue eyes is facing a group. I do the same.

Five men and a woman in dark blue jumpsuits with vests and helmets stand at the front of the line, all in FBI markings. Another six men in DEA vests fill in behind them, along with two men in blue windbreakers and ball caps marked ICE. At the back of the crowd, a pair of men in all black have bolt-action rifles with scopes. Cripes. Snipers? Good thing I have a giant yellow FBI logo on my back and chest. (HUD isn't issued military grade armor.) I hide my anxiety well and take a position beside Chad. It's hard not to think about Tammy and Anthony, and how they're safe at Mary Lou's house, unaware of the danger I'm about to hurl myself into.

I close my eyes and meditate on my training. Phantoms don't exist. Eerie feelings don't mean anything more than a manifestation of anxiety. Little kids sometimes have imaginary friends. Damn, please don't let an 'evil' imaginary friend mean my daughter's got real mental problems.

"Good afternoon everyone. For those of you who don't know me, I'm Special Agent William Martin. Our primary objective here is to serve an arrest warrant on Juan Manuel Villero, take him and any associates into custody, and have everyone walk away alive."

Nods and murmurs of agreement come from the group.

"At this time, we believe that Mr. Villero and six other adults are in the residence." Agent Martin gestures to his right, down the street. "Capriati and Walters, you'll go in and set up on the north and south sides respectively. Once you're emplaced, the rest of us will move in."

The snipers nod.

I swallow the saliva gathering in my mouth and fold my arms in case my hands decide to start shaking. We're all carrying weapons that can go straight through several houses in a row, especially these kinds of houses. I chant 'check your target' over and over in my mind. If I have to fire this M4, I need to be aware of what's behind the suspect. This is the worst part, right before. Once we're moving, I know my training will take over. Right here, thinking about everything that could go wrong, is when the nerves fray. In the heat of the moment, I'll be fine.

Special Agent Martin proceeds to assign everyone to positions. Chad and I get the rear of the house, along with the rest of our HUD fellows. We're going to head in along the road that runs behind the place and cover the backyard for runners.

The snipers jog off on foot, one cutting to the right between two houses. An FBI tech comes by and gets us all set up with earbuds and throat mics. Once we're all on the same channel, we pile into one of the Suburbans and wait. Radio chatter from the snipers confirms they are in position about five minutes later; Capriati is up a power line tower 180 yards from the south face of the house and Walters is on the roof of a two-story building 210 yards north.

"We are go," says Martin.

Montoya cuts across open dirt and down a slight hill before hanging a left on pavement, bouncing over the sidewalk. Rosa's house comes up fast on our left, and he pulls to a stop half off the road. Thirty yards of uphill littered with scrub brush and a few trees separates us from the backyard fence. I hop out and bring my M4 up to point in the general direction of the home, finger tight to the housing above the trigger well. In seconds, I mentally plot a path from tree to tree to the fence.

Capriati's behind us, observing the area through his rifle scope. He announces he's seen us, and says the back yard looks empty.

"Confirm two individuals in the front room,"

says Walters, the other sniper. "A woman and an unidentified man."

"Door team into position, yard team close in," says Martin.

We rush forward in a line, fanning out among the sparse trees. I run up to the nearest, bracing my shoulder against it while covering the slope ahead. Chad hustles up to another tree. As soon as his rifle's up, I fast-walk to the next tree.

"Ringing the doorbell in three... two... one..." says an unfamiliar man.

"FBI!" shouts the same guy in the distance. "Everyone down!"

I rush out from behind the last tree before the fence, which is chest-high to me. All of us climb over it with ease and stand there for a second or two observing the windows and back door of the residence. Men's shouting accompanies a woman's screams inside, but nothing moves in any window I have eyes on.

The others around me start advancing, leaving me a few steps back. Movement pulls my attention to the right, at a cluster of thick twelve-foot tall bushes against the side fence, which is much taller than the part we entered. A dirty, white sneaker sits in mulch, beneath a pant leg of camouflage cloth. Bryce, the farthest of us on that side, walked right past it.

That's not an abandoned shoe; it's a guy hiding.

I swivel, training my M4 in that direction. "Federal agent! You, out of the bushes. Get on the ground."

Chad, Bryce, and Michelle whirl around to look.

The bushes explode in a flurry of leaves as *two* young men bolt forward, both in green camouflage jackets and pants. One cuts left into a sprint for the rear fence while the second looks me right in the eye. At a flash of silver in his hand, I react on instinct and squeeze the trigger.

Our guns go off at the same time.

A hit like a baseball bat catches me in the left breast, knocking all the air out of my lungs. The guy twists to his left, a flash of fire spitting from the end of his pistol, but I have no idea where his second bullet went. The distant *bang* of a sniper rifle reaches my ears a half-second later. Staggering back and to my right, I fire again, wheezing, unable to breathe. My shoulder hits the ground at the same instant a ripple of gunfire goes off behind me, but I'm pretty sure my fellow agents lit up a standing corpse.

The one who shot me collapses in a heap.

Sprawled on the ground, I shift aim to the runner and try to yell "Stop!" but only make a sickly rasp of air.

Chad takes off after the guy, clearing the fence like a hurdle jumper.

Michelle runs up on the suspect and kicks the handgun away from him, keeping her rifle trained. A second later, she stoops and puts two fingers to his neck. "One suspect down. He's still breathing."

"Agent hit," yells Bryce over the radio. He skids

to a halt beside me. "Sam, you okay?"

I pat the vest and give a thumbs up. A porcelain-like shatter comes from the house, along with more men shouting. Scuffing and thumping beyond the fence makes me picture Chad and the runner tumbling down the hill.

Bryce helps me stand up. "Welcome to the club."

"You've…" I gasp. "You've been shot before?"

He nods. "Twice. Once without a vest, but it was a little .22."

"Not so little when you're hit," I say. Rubbing the vest doesn't ease the pain much, but I do it anyway out of reflex. "Might have a cracked rib."

Chad appears at the back of the yard, dragging a delirious Hispanic man with a bloody nose. He looks young, barely twenty, and flops like a rag doll when Chad hoists him over the fence. At least my partner doesn't throw the handcuffed guy face-first into the dirt. After handing him off to Montoya, he hurries over to me.

"Sam…"

"I'm fine. Vest took it." I glance out the corner of my eye at the wounded man. "Did I…"

Chad shakes his head. "You got him in the hip and the shoulder. Think you're still pushing when you fire."

He's probably right. I had that issue on the range. The M4 has barely any recoil, yet I still anticipate a big kick when firing, so I wind up hitting the target low. "Yeah. Guess I need more range time." Maybe it's not the kick at all, but my hesitance at having to kill someone? I don't think any cop, or federal agent for that matter, really thinks about that until the instant they're faced with a second or two in which to decide who dies. For my family, I can't hesitate, and I know I won't. That flash of silver, the suspect's sudden motion, replays in my mind over and over. My reaction had been devoid of thought or evaluation, a conditioned response. I couldn't have fired any faster unless I'd stormed in here looking to shoot anything that moved. That bastard was fast. Wonder how many hours he'd spent standing in front of a mirror practicing his cowboy quick draw.

Radio chatter from Agent Martin declares the area secure, and calls in an ambulance.

Chad claps me on the shoulder. "Good eyes. We all missed those two."

"The other one resist arrest?" I flick the safety back on, and hang the rifle on my right shoulder.

"Yep." He looks me over. "You hurt?"

"Sore. Probably a broken rib." A twinge of pain along my left side confirms just that when I try to breathe too deep.

He pokes around the spot, making me wince and gasp. "Hmm. Probably only bruised. Or you've got an inhuman pain tolerance."

"Or I'm still full of adrenaline." I smirk.

The FBI swarms the house while we stand guard. Pain throbs in my side, but it's more distracting than worrisome. As long as I don't take giant gulps of air or move faster than a deliberate walk, I can even keep a straight face. Ugh. Danny is going to go nuts tonight. He hates seeing me with a cold, and the idea that I'd been shot is going to launch him right off the deep end.

After the FBI removes Villero, three gang members, and one dead gang member from the house, we walk inside to check the place out. It's a two-bedroom single-story that makes my home feel huge. Aside from some fast food cartons in the living room and a smashed glass door on the entertainment center, the house looks well-kept, but sparse. One of the bedrooms has a folding table with scales, bags of white powder, and smaller bags lined up in a shallow cardboard tray. No piles of cash lying around though.

I stiff-leg it back to the living room where Rosa Melendez is seated on the couch, a frizz of carpet clinging to her cheek. She's barefoot, in a simple coral-colored dress clingy enough to show she's carrying no concealed weapons. Long, straight black hair hangs down enough to cover the handcuffs on her wrists behind her back. She looks both terrified and relieved. When we approach, she peers up at us with huge, brown eyes.

"Miss Melendez? I'm Agent Moon, and this is Agent Helling. We're federal investigators with the Department of Housing and Urban Development. We need to know about the nature of your relationship with Juan Villero."

"I have no choice. Please. I nothing to do with

this. They kill me if I say anything. Steal my house." Rosa trembles.

Chad takes out a notepad and scribbles. "How much of a cut did you get from this operation?"

Rosa shakes her head. "I nothing. They took the room. I cannot say no. I get no money. They only give me bruises. Worse if I tell police what they do here."

I'm inclined to believe her. It's difficult to fake the fear in her eyes, though I suppose she could be terrified of deportation. She hasn't been naturalized yet. "How long have they been here? Why did they pick you?"

Rosa holds eye contact. "I coming from work last May. At night in parking lot, a man grabs me from behind with a gun. I afraid he rape me, but he no. Makes me drive him here, to my home. Looks around like he checking it to buy, and tells me he using the room for his people, or they shoot me."

"Last May?" asks Chad. "So, three months?"

Rosa shakes her head. "No. A year ago."

I would sit next to her for this question, but not with my throbbing rib. Still, I lower my voice as sympathetic as I can get. "Rosa... were you sexually assaulted?"

She stares down.

"Shit," whispers Chad.

I grit my teeth in pain while stooping forward, and unlock her cuffs. She's a victim here. I'm sure the FBI thought so too, since they didn't cart her off with the others. Still, abused women have been known to go nuts and attack the police who show up to arrest their husbands. I understand why they left her restrained, but the scene is secure now, and she's terrified.

Rosa folds her hands in her lap, rubbing her wrists. "*Gracias.*"

"We'd like you to come to our office and give a statement. Umm… *Declaración del testigo*. At this time, you aren't being charged with anything. *No se le está cobrando.*"

She bows her head. "They have people all over Los Angeles. In Mexico, too. They will take revenge if I tell you."

"These guys barged in and made you a prisoner in your own home." Chad scowls at the rug. "If you help us out, maybe you stop this from happening to someone else."

Rosa fidgets.

"Think about it a moment, okay?" I force a smile past my aching side.

DEA agents stream in and out the front door with boxes. I lope over to the kitchen and look around. It's neat and tidy, suggesting the thugs didn't force her to cook for them. That this property went through HUD doesn't strike me as being a factor in the gang's operation. More likely, they preyed on a woman who they knew they could intimidate, and would be hesitant to go to the authorities. Some green card holders are afraid a simple parking ticket might get their permanent resident status revoked. Despite public perception, most of the people we work with are born here.

A white business card on the fridge catches my eye. It bears a phone number in the middle, with 'Marty' written in sharpie marker below. I tug it out from under its magnet and take short steps back to the living room.

"Rosa?" I hold out the card. "Is this yours or theirs?"

She looks up at the card for a second before again looking me in the eye. "It's mine."

"Who's Marty?" I ask.

Rosa shrugs and waves dismissively. "He is a fixing man. If the sink or toilet stop working, he makes it good again."

"Ahh. All right." There are quite a few guys that troll these areas looking for work like that. More than a few of them undocumented. Might come in handy as leverage down the line, since unlicensed work on a HUD property could violate her agreement. Still, this woman's had a rough time of it and I don't have any desire to make her life even worse. I hand the card to Chad. "Would you mind putting that back on the fridge?"

"Sure." He takes it, tilting it in the light to read it.

"Miss Melendez," I say, "if you'd like to speak with someone who helps women who've been assaulted, we can arrange that for you at no cost." A flash of pain in my side makes me shudder, but I grit my teeth, trying not to let it show on my face. "And a medical evaluation if you'd like."

Rosa looks up at me.

"Speaking of medical evaluations." Chad grasps my right arm above the elbow. "We can interview Miss Melendez in a couple days."

Grr. He's got a point, as much as I hate admitting it. "All right. Please think about that counseling."

Rosa nods.

Chad guides me outside. We hand the M4s in at the FBI truck, and I lean against it while he jogs off to get our car from where we left it two blocks east. Agent Martin, standing by the street amid a cluster of other FBI personnel, spots me and hurries over.

"Agent Moon, what are you still doing here? Weren't you hit?"

I grimace, nod, and point at the impact spot on the vest. "Wasn't quite done yet."

He chuckles. "I wish half my team was that dedicated. Still. You need to get checked out. I can get your debrief from Fortunato later. As soon as you feel up to it, send him your report of what happened back there. If there are any gaps that need to be filled, someone from my team will stop by."

"Sure." I can't quite smile, feeling light-headed. Not sure if it's pain or that I've been sipping air instead of really breathing.

Special Agent Martin helps me to the car when Chad pulls up. "Are you sure you don't want an ambulance?"

"Chad's already here." My eyes bug out from pain when I slide into the seat. Maybe a stretcher would've been a better idea after all. Still… the idea of getting out of the car hurts enough to keep me planted.

"Okay. Straight to the hospital," says Martin to Chad, before closing my door.

"Ugh." I lean my head back. "Danny's going to lose his mind."

Chapter Six
Lucky

As it turned out, I walked away from being shot with two bruised ribs. They probably would've cracked if the guy had a magnum, but he only had a .45. Still, the doctor estimated about three weeks for the pain to stop. This, of course, resulted in Fortunato ordering me to stay home for at least a full week.

I called Danny and Mary Lou one after the next, explaining I'd be getting home a little late due to work. Of the two, my husband got the truth of *why* I was late, and predictably freaked. Since my sister had all the kids to watch, I didn't need her panicking. The X-ray and exam chewed up a couple hours, and Chad dropped me off at home around seven. By the time I walked in the door, the pain meds kicked in enough to reduce my agony to strong discomfort.

Danny went into full nurse mode as soon as he saw the giant bruise from my armpit to the base of my ribcage. My left boob went purple due to subdermal bleeding, but it should clear up in a few days. Good thing Anthony's been off breast milk for a while. I don't even want to think about how much that would hurt now.

My sister also flipped when she found out I'd been shot. She and Danny flew around the house like dervishes, taking care of things while I lay like a beached whale on the sofa, barely able to sit up. Tammy gave me a welcome home present of jumping into a hug, which hurt so much I had a whiteout. By the time I could see again, Danny had plucked her off me and explained that I'd been hurt and needed some 'no pouncing' time. Once Tammy understood, she cuddled up on my unbruised side like a living teddy bear. A four-year-old can't do much around the house to help, but this kid gave up her playtime to comfort me. I cried for a good hour after I realized what she was doing. Talk about guilt. Not that she meant it in that way, but I couldn't stop thinking about all the what-ifs, like not having a vest on or if the guy had shot me in the face.

Two days later, Nico paid me a visit at home to get my version of what happened on the raid. The whole thing was still as clear in my mind as if it had happened only minutes before.

So, yeah... a few days doing nothing but watching television while clinging to my daughter wasn't boring at all. I savored every second of still being alive.

***

It's been almost a week since the raid, and I'm still sore as hell. At least I can take a full breath again. The hardest part about this has been resting and trying not to do anything physical. I never realized how mind-numbingly awful daytime television is—except for *Judge Judy*. Mary Lou brought her three kids over during the day all week long, and even gave me the first three seasons of *Judge Judy* on DVD, a lifeline, since watching actual daytime TV made me feel like an old woman.

Tammy keeps up her habit of cuddling by my good side, just being there, hoping she's helping me feel better. Every few hours, I make sure she knows she is.

Around one, suspicious giggling from the inner hallway gets me worrying. Mary Lou's passed out in the recliner, Tammy's tucked up beside me staring at cartoons, and the rest of the children are in the back, probably Anthony's room.

"Ellie Mae?" I call. "Everything okay?"

Silence is *not* the correct response.

When the giggling starts up again, I glance over at my sister, who's seriously passed out. I feel bad bothering her since she's been working her ass off between helping me and taking care of her household too. I grit my teeth and stand, leaving

Tammy on the couch, and wobble down the hallway.

Anthony darts across the hallway from his room to Tammy's, naked, and covered in marker doodles. Seconds later, Billy Joe, my sister's four-year-old son, streaks by, also wearing only marker scrawls.

"Get back here!" yells Ellie Mae, from Anthony's room.

Ruby Grace, the two-year-old, babbles something about diapers.

I amble up to where the two bedrooms stand across the hall from each other, then look left and right.

On the left, Anthony and Billy Joe square off like a pair of drunken fencers, jabbing at each other with colored markers. On the right, Ellie Mae's kneeling in the middle of Anthony's room in her underpants, marker smears across her chest. Her dress hangs from the doorknob, mercifully clean, and a diaper holding an unspeakable mess lays out in all its glory in front of her. Ruby Grace, the perfect picture of an innocent bystander, is hip-deep in Anthony's pile of stuffed animals. No marker, and all her clothes are where they belong.

"What's going on?" I ask, leaning on the doorjamb for balance.

"Anthony messed his diaper." Ellie Mae points across the hall. "Mommy's asleep, so I had ta change him, but he runned off after wipies."

"Why is your dress on the doorknob?"

She blinks at me like I asked a dumb question.

"So it don't get any poop on it."

I glance at Tammy's room where the boys continue their marker duel. "Why is your brother naked?"

Ellie Mae shrugs. "I dunno. He get in trouble if he got marker on his clothes."

Ahh, the joys of children.

"Go wash your hands and get dressed."

Ellie Mae scrambles off to the bathroom while I stoop to collect the diaper, groaning from the flare up in my side. The mess is abnormally aromatic today, making my eyes water. What the hell has Danny been feeding him? The boys, giggling their heads off, run back in.

"Stop that." I grab the markers and re-cap them. Since they've already gotten undressed, I take them by the hand to the bathroom. Ellie Mae darts by, her hands dripping wet, and scurries into Anthony's room while Ruby Grace continues to frolic in the mountain of plushies.

"Sam?" asks Mary Lou from the living room end of the hall. "What happened?"

If I wasn't nursing a bruised rib, I'd have held her son up by one arm like a caught fish. Instead, I merely maneuver him so she can get a good look at the marker scrawls. "Zorro lost."

"Oh, I'm sorry… I fell asleep and—"

"Stop apologizing," I say. "You're overextending yourself."

Mary Lou runs over and takes the boys' hands. "I got it. Go lie down, you're still hurt."

Ellie Mae, back in her dress, steps out into the hall, faces her mother, and beams. "I changed Anthony! He made a pock lips."

My look of stunned confusion gets my sister laughing.

"Ricky calls a loaded diaper 'an apocalypse.'" She tugs the boys into the bathroom. "Come on, you two. Bath time." Halfway in the door, she peers back at me. "Sam, are these water soluble?"

I hold them up in a fist, grinning. "The boy's two. *Everything* is water soluble."

Ellie Mae follows me back to the living room to watch TV.

"Sorry for waking Aunt Marlou up," says Tammy. "You need to be not moving so you get not hurt faster."

I ruffle her hair. "Thank you."

The rest of the day passes in relative calm. At least as calm as can be expected with five children aged six and younger around. Ricky, my sister's husband, arrives at 5:45 p.m., dying to hear about my 'shootout.' Tammy stares up at me wide-eyed. I hadn't told her *how* I got hurt. Ugh. Her gaze turns pleading.

"Yeah." I pull her into a hug. "A bad guy shot at me, but I had a vest on."

She clings.

Ricky cringes. "Oops."

I sigh. "It's all right. She was going to find out sooner or later."

Mary Lou starts cooking, baked chicken and

mashed potatoes from the smell of it, and soon after Danny gets home at six, we all collect around the table. Danny and Ricky kibitz about work, mostly about how Ricky is considering starting up his own electrician business instead of working for a company, and wants Danny's opinion since he's gone independent already.

"Cai have more a'tatoes?" asks Billy Joe.

Anthony grabs a handful off his plate and throws it at him before I can react, nailing the boy square in the face. Billy Joe appears not to mind this, and scoops the splatter into his mouth. Mary Lou jumps up to wipe him down while Danny whisper-scolds Anthony.

Despite the dull ache in my side, I couldn't be happier, surrounded by family. This is going to be one of those memories that will stick with me forever. A few snapped photos from my cell phone won't hurt either, right? I snap Anthony, his face covered by little bits of mashed potatoes and gravy making goofy faces across the table at Ruby Grace. Next photo is Ellie Mae trying her best not to get any food on her pretty little dress. I get one of Tammy, a look of stern concentration shoving her eyebrows together as she tries to figure out how the whole using a fork thing works. A few more snaps capture Ricky and Danny laughing and Mary Lou looking exhausted but fulfilled.

The guys graciously clean up after the meal. We hang out for a bit after, but it's not long before Mary Lou gives Rick the 'it's time' glance. I grunt and push myself up to stand, which causes Danny to run over and try to get me to sit back down.

"I'm okay. It's getting better." I kiss him before drifting over to the door as Mary Lou is matching shoes to children. "Hey. Thank you so much for all this help. Soon as I'm back to a hundred percent, I'm going to take a week off work and watch your three."

"Oh, it's all right. You just did take a week off work." Mary Lou gingerly hugs me. "I should've become a teacher or something. Watching kids *is* fun for me."

Rick picks Ruby Grace up and sets her standing in her itty-bitty sneakers. "You look exhausted, hon," he says to Mary Lou. "Maybe you should listen to your sister. We haven't been away for a long time, just us."

"Well, I'll think about it. Don't want Sam getting in trouble. She hasn't been at her job that long." Mary Lou hugs Danny, counts kids, and heads out with a, "See you tomorrow."

I push the door closed and lean my forehead against it. I hate needing to be taken care of like this. My sister did plenty of that when we were kids. I'm the strong-willed one. There's no reason I need to stay out of work another week. It's not fair to her. Plus, I got bad guys to catch.

"Sam?" Danny walks up behind me, placing a hand on my shoulder. "What's wrong?"

I turn away from the door and cling to him. "Just feeling like a burden. I think I'm going to go in Monday."

"You're not a burden." Danny kisses me. "Though, you know I've been wondering if I could talk you into doing something less dangerous."

"I'm *fine*, Danny. Ninety-nine days out of a hundred, I stare at paperwork."

He gazes into my eyes, pain and worry etched in new lines on his face. "Yeah, but all it takes is one day... one moment."

I look down.

After an awkward silence, Danny sighs. "I'm not going to force you to make any decisions. This is just me being worried to death."

He pulls me close, holding me for a few minutes in silence. Being a federal agent is something I busted my ass for, and giving it up over some punk drug runner isn't gonna happen. It'll take a lot worse than a bruised rib to make me walk away from everything I put into getting this job. I'd be lying if I said I wasn't keenly aware of the risk, more so than ever. Tammy's reaction almost did it. If that kid ever asks me to 'stop getting shot at' or something like that, I very well might cave in. Last week was an anomaly. The odds are in my favor as a federal agent, especially with HUD. Beat cops have it far worse. Maybe in a couple years, I can transfer to the FBI and investigate corporate fraud or something along those lines. I'm not gung-ho like Bryce. I'll be happy as long as I'm still a federal agent.

"I'm really lucky to have you, Danny Moon." I

lean up and kiss him deeply on the lips.

He runs his hands down my back and squeezes my ass. I moan into his mouth. My side's tender, but I'm willing to put up with a little soreness for this. We've both been so busy lately, it's been almost a month since we had sex.

Anthony's shout of, "Daddy! I potty!" pours a bucket of ice water over the mood.

We crack up laughing into each other's shoulders.

Soon, our son runs in wearing only a shirt, grinning from ear to ear. "I did it!"

He leads us back to the bathroom to show off the little potty chair with most of the pee in its basin. Most. There are dribbles on the wall, the side of the sink, and the floor as well.

"Very good!" Danny scoops him up and swings him around. When he faces me again, he mouths, "I'll clean it" without lending it voice, and carries the boy off to bed.

I collect Tammy and tuck her in. After goodnight kisses, Danny and I sneak back to the living room and wind up on the couch together.

"Feels like I'm in high school worried my dad's going to walk in and catch us," says Danny.

"Hah," I laugh. "Mine would've kept on walking like nothing was going on."

Danny threads his arm around behind me and carefully pulls me closer. "Seriously? He wouldn't have freaked out?"

"Depends on the year. Junior or senior, he

probably wouldn't have made a big deal out of it. Free love and all that. As long as the guy was close to my age."

"Is two years older too much?" Danny eyes me up and down. "I'm having pretty impure thoughts right now."

I bite my lip and trace a finger across his jaw-line. "That's not much of a difference. He'd be more worried that you're a lawyer. Tools of 'the system,' much like federal agents."

Danny leans his head into mine. "Your parents are being foolish like mine."

"They think you've sold your soul, too?"

He chuckles. "Hah. No... my soul's staying right where it is, thank you very much. But they never fail to miss a chance to remind me how much it's in danger for having married a woman who doesn't go to church."

"Ugh. Parents."

"Parents." He nods.

"I'm glad I have you, Danny. I have no need of judgmental people in my life."

He puts a finger under my chin and lifts my head into a kiss. "There's nothing in this world more important to me than you."

"We're not going to turn out like our parents, are we? Our kids breaking off contact and not wanting to see us?" Well, technically, Danny's parents don't mind seeing *him*. It's me they don't want around.

"No, we're not." He smiles. "You're the most

devoted mommy in the world. Our kids could turn out to both be serial killers and you'd still smother them with love."

I roll into him, muffling my laughter against his chest. "That's not even funny."

"Sorry," he says. "We both know Anthony's a perfect angel, and Tammy's her mother's shadow. Your sister's words, not mine. She also says our kids are a bit backwards."

"Backwards how?" I raise an eyebrow.

"Something about daughters usually glomming onto their fathers and sons hanging onto their mother's leg."

I snuggle tighter to him. "They're still small."

Minutes later, the snuggling turns into something a little more than snuggling. My hand brushes against something rigid. "Oh, someone's awake."

Danny places a gentle hand over my injured side. "Maybe we shouldn't? I don't want to hurt you."

Unable to help myself, I laugh. "It's not *that* big."

He stares at me.

I laugh some more. "Come on. I'm teasing."

Danny scoops me up and lifts me into the air. "Not that big, eh?" he asks in a bad attempt at an old Dick Tracy voice. "Well, I'll show you a thing or two!"

Trying not to giggle loud enough to wake the kids, I kick my feet and fake pound at his back as he carries me down the hall to our bedroom.

Chapter Seven
Trust

Friday, I'm up and able to do something I haven't pulled off in ages: cook breakfast. Too much sitting around has left me an abundance of energy. We have a (relatively) quick family breakfast before Danny rushes off to work, nearly colliding with Mary Lou on the path to the driveway. Her two oldest zoom in the door and begin running in circles around the sofa. Tammy, cheering, pursues. Ruby Grace dangles, squirming from my sister's arms until the front door closes, and toddles off into the frenzy once her mother puts her down.

Anthony slaps his high chair shelf and yells, "Go-be-down."

"What are you doing?" Mary Lou hurries over and gawps at me.

"Cleaning up after breakfast, what's it look

like?" I grin.

"You're…" She relaxes. "You look better."

"Well my side's still sore, but I'm *so* done with sitting on my ass all day."

Mary Lou hugs me, still quite careful not to squeeze too hard. "Don't overdo it."

"I'm good. Going back to the office Monday."

"So soon? But the doctor said three weeks!" Mary Lou glances up from wiping pancake syrup off Anthony's chair.

"What can I say? I heal fast."

Ellie Mae walks in. "Aunt Sam, can we watch cartoons?"

"Of course, sweetie."

"Yay!" Ellie May zips off to the living room.

I duck in to turn the TV on and return to my sink of dishwater.

"I'm really glad to see you doing so well." Mary Lou smiles and tosses a wad of paper towels in the trash, having made quick work of the syrupy mess.

My arms up to the elbows in hot suds, I say, "Chad called to check up on me last night. The suspect who shot me's only sixteen."

Mary Lou gasps. "Oh, that's…"

"He's not dead like I thought. Chad said he's expected to make it, but they're not sure if he'll ever walk again." I pick the egg pan out of the water and attack it with a sponge. "As soon as I realized I didn't watch someone die, it felt like a huge weight fell off my shoulders."

"Sam…" Mary Lou leans against the counter

beside me. "He tried to kill you. I mean, it's *awful* that he's so young, but… these people have a different life."

"These people?" I quirk an eyebrow at her. "You're starting to sound like Dad."

Mary Lou gazes at the ceiling, sighing. "Not that kind of 'these people.' I don't mean it as a racial thing. How could I? You never even told me what he looked like. I mean these drug dealer gangs. They recruit them young and these poor kids don't know any different. Trafficking and killing become a way of life."

"I guess." My mind drifts back to his expression in the instant before muzzle flash bloomed in front of his face. Panic. I don't think he really wanted to do anything but get away. "Still. It's a lot easier to sleep knowing I didn't kill anyone."

"Didn't you say the sniper got him?" asks Mary Lou.

"Seemed like it at the time. This heavy *boom* went off somewhere behind me and the kid spins around and drops."

"Aww." Mary Lou gives me a quick hug before moving to wipe down the table. She glances back at me, opens her mouth, and looks down.

"What?" I ask.

"Oh, nothing. Just… I umm. Don't want you to get hurt. If someone points a gun at you—"

"I did get hurt." I set the pan in the drainer. "But I didn't hesitate either. I'm just not a great shot with a carbine."

"Mom! Wipies!" shouts Billy Joe from the bathroom.

We laugh.

"Wow that didn't take long." I wink at my sister. "You haven't been here twenty minutes yet."

Ellie Mae darts into the bathroom.

"No. I want Mommy!" yells Billy Joe. "Go 'way!"

Mary Lou walks off to deal with her son while I finish off the kitchen and flop on the couch. Tammy crawls up to sit next to me again, grinning. I think she knows I'm feeling better, but she still wants to tuck under my arm.

I deal with some light housework and laundry, though Mary Lou insists on carrying the baskets for me still. It's a nice day out, so we set the kids loose in the front yard for a while before lunch. Later, with them all (mostly) down for naptime, I flip on *Judge Judy*.

Mary Lou emerges from the hallway after coaxing Ruby Grace to sleep (that kid has an inhuman amount of energy) and arrives at the couch by way of the kitchen. She hands me a bottle of iced tea, opens hers, and takes a huge gulp. "This is good, but it's missing something."

"Bit early for vodka."

"Blasphemy." She chuckles, but her mirth melts away to a worried look.

She's got our father's longish nose, and when she's moody, sad, or anxious, she turns into a (much) prettier version of him with long hair. I wouldn't say Dad's nose is *too* long, but I will say I'm glad I got Mom's.

"What's bothering you? And before you say nothing, you look like Dad in a wig again."

She barks a laugh like a startled hen. "Oh, that's not fair. Okay fine." She stares down at her lap. "I'm worried Ricky might be cheating on me."

My attempt to take a sip of tea turns into a coughing fit. Oh, damn, that hurts. I lean back, holding my side and cringing.

"Sorry! Sorry!" she says, realizing what she'd done. "Never mind."

I wag my finger at her. "No take-backs on something like that. You got some splainin' ta do."

"Your Ricky Ricardo is horrible." Mary Lou rubs my shoulder. "Are you okay?"

"Yeah. Coughing is not a good thing for me yet. And thus far, my experiments to breathe tea have proven unsuccessful." I fix her with a serious look. "Why on Earth do you think he's cheating? Ricky?! I can't believe it."

"Well." She stares at the label on her drink, twisting the bottle around and around in her hands.

Appropriately enough, Judge Judy is reaming out some idiot for taking his girlfriend's car without permission and getting into a minor accident. Her rant began when he slipped and admitted he was on his way to his *other* girlfriend's place at the time.

"Out with it, Mary Lou."

She looks up at me. "He's come home really late twice this week. Tuesday and Wednesday. Both times, he said the guys from work wanted to hang out. But… he's been with Harris Electric for almost six years and he's never 'gone out with the guys' before."

"I have a hard time believing Ricky would do that to you. He doesn't seem like that kind of man."

"They never do." She closes her eyes to hold back tears.

"Hey." I grasp her hand. "Maybe he finally feels secure enough at the job to do something like that, or maybe one of the guys is retiring or getting married or quitting and they're celebrating. Did you talk to him about it?"

She gasps. "No. What if I'm wrong and he really is going out with the boys? I don't want to turn into *that* wife who flips out if her man doesn't spend every waking second at her side. I'd sound paranoid."

"Okay. Has anything else happened, or has he just been late twice?" I hold up my tea. "Before you answer that, let me take a sip."

She grins, but waits for me to lower the bottle. "Well, he seemed a little odd the first night. Avoided looking me in the eye, and wound up clingy."

"Maybe he thought you were mad at him for going out?" I wink.

"The second time he came back…" Mary Lou lowers her voice to almost a whisper. "He had a red mark on the side of his neck."

I blink. "Seriously? A hickey?"

"Well." She kneads her hands into her skirt. "I didn't get a good look at it, but it could be. He was trying to keep me from seeing it."

"You've always been the protector, and I've always been the one who could read people." I nudge her. "I don't think Ricky would do that to you."

She gives me the meekest look I've ever seen on her before. "What if was Danny? How would you handle it if you thought he cheated on you?"

I stare into space. Other than being utterly crushed? I can't even imagine my Danny going behind my back with another woman. We're as close as the cliché gets to soul mates. I—it's incomprehensible to the point my brain refuses to even ponder the hypotheticals. "He'd never do that," I finally say.

"See?" Mary Lou sighs. "You can't think objectively. You and Danny are so perfect together."

"So are you and Ricky. He *adores* you and the kids."

Judge Judy's voice at the edge of my consciousness scolding the guy for betraying his girlfriend gets my guts in a knot. If Danny did anything like that, I'd make the judge's tirade seem tame. Whether or not that happened before or after I spent weeks in a deep, dark place, I can't say. Though, I know Danny would never betray me. Confident in what we have, I smile inwardly.

"I know... I know," says my sister. "He's

always been so sweet. That's why it's so weird that he's being evasive."

"How's he being evasive?" I ask.

"He has a tell."

"A tell?"

"You know, like poker players," said Mary Lou. "Let me explain. A couple years ago, his parents wanted to come down from Oklahoma and spend like two weeks. Billy Joe'd been home from the hospital only for a day or three, and they wanted to help with the new baby."

Ricky's parents are like six-foot-tall redneck toddlers on a blend of crack cocaine and caffeine. Friendly as hell, but they have strong personalities and a weak sense of personal boundaries. Their son's an electrician and you'd think he invented the Space Shuttle. His parents still worry about using electrical appliances because they don't want to 'drain too much lightning outta the sky.' They're sweet, but simple… and *opinionated.* Visiting for a day or two, okay. Two weeks? Ack!

I cringe.

"Yeah, exactly how we felt. So, Ricky made up this cockamamie story of Billy Joe havin' some kinda delicate immune system issue and he needed at least a couple weeks before he could be exposed to other people. Well, he was straight up lying to them, right, and his lips kept twitchin' to the side. When he told me he'd been out with the boys, his lips did the same thing."

Hmm. "Maybe he's setting up some kinda

surprise for you?" I smile.

"Or something." She huffs. "You know I should maybe hire one of those private investigators to watch him."

"Now you're really getting paranoid." I poke her in the side. "What you should do, is talk to him. What a concept!"

"Yeah." Mary Lou averts her gaze, a sure sign she's going to ignore my advice.

Ruby Grace wobbles into the room. From the way she's walking, I know right away she's carrying cargo. She comes to a halt by Mary Lou and fixes her with a serious look. Her fine light brown hair catches the sunlight, glowing like an aura. After a dramatic pause, she lifts her dress to show off her diaper. And, with a vocabulary beyond her years, says, "This is squishy and totally unacceptable."

I crack up.

"It's not funny." Ruby Grace shifts her attention to me. "Poop is not funny when it's stuck to your butt. It's unfortunate. No one likes poop stuck to their butt."

Oh, cruel child, making me laugh. With tears in my eyes, I cradle my bruised rib and careen over sideways, trying to stop. Mary Lou collects her daughter and heads off down the hall. Anthony and Tammy walk in, both yawning.

"I made potty but it's nothing there," says Anthony.

It takes me a second to piece together he

attempted to use the potty, but still had his diaper in the way. Ugh. I need a changing table for two. "Come on, little man."

Hey, I might as well go back to work on Monday. Either way, I'm dealing with poop.

8.
Stealth

Saturday evening after the kids are sleeping, I cuddle up against Danny's side on the couch.

I've already called Nico and told him I'm going to be in Monday. He sounded concerned, but open to the idea. Desk work shouldn't be too bad. If, by some odd chance, the FBI calls in another favor, I'm sure he'll insist I sit it out. But I'm not sparing even two brain cells to work at the moment. Mary Lou's worries about Ricky have me being uncharacteristically clingy.

The TV's on, but neither of us are paying much attention to it. For the past half hour or so, he's been giving me the 'what did I do?' look. I've been too preoccupied with him to care what's happening on the idiot box.

"Okay, I give up. What?" Danny glances down at my both arms wrapped around his left.

"Can't I hold my husband?"

He grins. "Of course, but you're not usually this… possessive."

I shrug. "We've spent the past year and change burning the candle at both ends. My head's finally stopped spinning." I snuggle up to him and randomly stick my nose in his ear. He squirms and chuckles, letting out an "Ow, hey!" when I nibble on his earlobe.

"Oh, I get it." Danny pulls me over so I'm lying with my back across his lap. "You're getting used to having a small army running around. You want to catch up to your sister."

I grin. "I dunno about a third, but I wouldn't mind a practice run."

"Is it the shooting?" He strokes my hair. A little worry tints his expression. "Whatever you decide to do, I'll support you all the way."

"Maybe a teeny bit, but…" I sigh, staring up at the ceiling… and a green marker squiggle. "Mary Lou said something unnerving, and *how* did Anthony write on the ceiling?"

Danny leans his head back. "Wow. Kid's got talent."

"Ugh. We only painted two months ago. I hope that washes out. Water soluble means it only takes one coat of paint to hide it."

"Don't worry about it." He tickles my stomach,

making me curl up. Okay, that didn't hurt *too* much. Maybe a little. "I still have some of the paint in the garage. I'll touch it up tomorrow if it doesn't. So, what's bugging you?"

I explain Mary Lou's worry that Ricky might be cheating on her. "She even flirted with the idea of hiring a PI to tail him." I chuckle, although it comes out sounding more nervous than I'd intended.

"A PI isn't an unreasonable option, except for the fact we're discussing Mary Lou and Ricky here." He winks. "I just can't see him cheating."

"Me neither."

"I've used PIs before, for cases... They come in handy when I need to conceal my involvement until the documents are served. Last time, the guy dug up proof—credit card receipts and a witness statement—the other driver suing my client had been out drinking right before the accident. Here's a tip. If you want to keep a low profile, don't stiff your waitress on a tip. She remembered him like it just happened."

I chuckle. "Wow. Private investigators really exist? I thought that was just like a movie thing."

"Yeah, they're real, but the movies overdo it. From what I hear, the job's mostly internet searching, document sifting, and digging through trash these days... but I guess the stalking a cheater with a camera thing still happens sometimes. At least, for what I've needed them for, they've been a lifesaver. Basically handed us that case, for instance. But, I just can't see Ricky messing around."

"I can see *us* messing around." I trace my finger around in circles on his chest.

His grin widens. We lock lips for a while like a pair of horny teens before we migrate to the bedroom at the end of the hall and close the door. It doesn't take long for us to wind up naked, and Danny decides to play doctor, checking out my wounded boob. The bruising is almost gone from my breast, and it's not even sore to the touch. Enough purple remains on the skin right below it that he only gingerly brushes my ribs with his fingertips.

"It looks worse than it is," I whisper before leaning close and sucking on the side of his neck.

Danny lifts me back up onto the bed and slides up next to me. "You sound like most of my clients."

My lips break contact with his neck as I laugh, but I bite my finger to keep quiet. The kids and all that. Danny slides down, and the scratchiness of his beard settles between my thighs. Oh... I grab the sheets and stifle a moan. I never imagined Danny would be into anything more risqué than normal missionary, but he surprised me with how quick he became adventurous. I don't even remember who brought up the topic at some company party years ago, but the next time we wound up in bed I joked about it and... he didn't hesitate. We've even messed around with a little kink, but I've avoided anything involving handcuffs since Tammy started walking.

I am *not* explaining that to my kids. Anything that prevents or complicates a quick dive under the covers is off the table unless Danny and I have the house to ourselves. Judging from his enthusiasm at the moment, he doesn't really miss the kinky stuff.

After a few minutes of his attention, I'm writhing and grabbing at the sheets, doing everything I can to choke back the deep moan struggling to escape my throat. Sound happens involuntarily when he hits a spot that sends a lightning charge over my whole body. I clamp a pillow over my head to muffle my gasps and moans of ecstasy until Danny slides back up and pulls it aside.

"I'd ask if you're ready, but it's all over your face."

"That's not where it's going tonight," I say.

He raises an eyebrow. "I was kidding about number three."

Without looking, I fish a packet out of the nightstand. "I know."

Danny grins. After he puts on the condom, he warms me up a little more by kissing my neck and playing with my breasts. When he finally puts his weapon to use, I bite his shoulder and moan.

"When did you get so into biting?" whispers Danny.

"Since... I don't... want to wake... the kids."

He teases a finger across my lips. "Careful. You might start to *like* biting me."

"When did we wind up trying to do this as quiet

as possible? Feels like I'm sixteen again with a boy in my room." (Well, technically, it was mine and my sister's room.) The sensation of his skin moving against mine, of him inside me, twists my brain into a spiral of uselessness that isn't going to care about noise. If Danny keeps being this good, I may have to raid the 'black box' of toys I hid in the attic for a gag.

He slows and leans down to kiss my ear before whispering. "Since we became a family."

Something tells me I'm not going to get a lot of sleep tonight.

Chapter Nine
Secret Admirer

After a leisurely Sunday involving a mall trip, lunch out, and an hour or so of watching the kids play in the lawn sprinkler, I return to work Monday morning. Everyone notices the stiffness in my walk, though I don't explain why my ribs are sore again. Still, the night I had with Danny was worth it. The guys get me a bullet-shaped cake and someone even found the slug that bounced off my vest. It's in a jar on my desk.

Raúl Reyes, the sixteen-year-old who shot me, is still on life support but officially 'out of the woods.' Turns out, I hit him twice, once in the thigh and once in the shoulder. The sniper got him in the chest, but missed the heart by an inch—likely due to Michelle, Ernie, and Bryce all shooting him at the same time and making him twist. The poor kid took five 5.56 rounds plus a .308 from the sniper and he's still on this planet. I call that freak luck, but

I'm sure he's probably thinking God was involved. Heck, for all I know, maybe something like destiny or fate *did* happen.

Though, really, he's just lucky we brought an ambulance with us. If he had to wait for one to get there, he probably wouldn't have made it. Agent Martin expected drug runners dealing in hundreds of thousands of dollars at a time to be armed like the military of a small third-world country, but they only had a couple handguns… and our primary target, Villero, didn't even go for a weapon. Probably because one guy in the living room pointed a revolver at the door when it was bashed open, and died instantly.

ICE thought they 'got one,' but Reyes was born in LA. Rumor has it his parents are considering a lawsuit since 'their poor baby' didn't need to be shot so many times. I feel for them to a point since I'm sure they don't understand what their son had been involved in, but good damn luck suing the federal government after your son opened fire on an agent. This isn't some small-town police department that'll just settle out of court.

Anyway, Monday proves to be easy and boring. I spend the whole day at my desk except for the occasional trip to the bathroom. Chad's a saint and goes to pick up Chinese takeout for lunch. Geez. You'd think I had both legs in a cast or something.

Danny sends me a text at about three asking if I'd be up for a formal dinner party. A judgment came down on a lawsuit he'd been busting his ass on for months, and his guy won. Unusually enough, Danny's client wasn't the one who initiated the suit. The man's quite wealthy, and evidently suffered a heart attack behind the wheel and plowed into another car from behind after losing consciousness. The guy was hospitalized for months with severe injuries, but the old couple he rear-ended weren't so lucky. Both died. Their adult children tried to sue Danny's client, claiming he was negligent or some such bullshit. It looked obvious to me they were trying to shake the money tree. The son had a substantial list of arrests for petty theft, and the daughter's clean but not rolling in cash.

Anyway, the client invited Danny and Jeff, plus their two paralegals over for dinner to celebrate. Normally, I tend to expect wealthy people to be scumbags, (I blame my parents' constant rants) but this guy seemed genuinely nice. He initially offered to pay for all the funeral and medical expenses of the people he hit. Danny texts me that his client even repeated that offer in court after the verdict.

Okay. I guess not everyone with gobs of money's automatically a douche. I think I have something in the closet I can wear for this. I text back, "Okay, but let me check with Mary Lou first."

I'm really going to have to take her kids and have them move in with us for a month so my sister can have a vacation. She's the best. With her agreeing to watch Tammy and Anthony tonight, I shoot a quick text to Danny to let him know I'm good to go.

Rosa hasn't made contact as far as I can tell with either a counselor or Chad. I bet she's petrified. Grr. That poor woman. Having her home stolen out from under her and being assaulted repeatedly in her own bed? I wouldn't be surprised if she burned the place to ashes to cleanse her mind. Maybe by Wednesday, Nico will let me out of the office and we can go check on her.

The remainder of the day is a blur of auditing, mostly phase-ones as I call them. HUD tenants at their six-month mark, where I look for undeclared income, criminal activity, or anything else that violates their agreement and leaves a paper trail I can find from remote.

***

I've come to think of LA traffic as one of the inner rings of Hell.

The worst of the damned are condemned to drive up and down the freeway in endless rush hour. It's 6:18 p.m. by the time I get in the door at home, and Danny's pacing circles in the living room wearing a new-looking black suit. He starts to give me a 'where have you been' look, but my eyes are inches from firing Superman style lasers and melting something down.

"Traffic?" he asks, one eyebrow cocked.

"Yeah." Since I know the kids are still at my sister's, I throw my head back and yell, "God-damned morons! Argh!"

"Got you something." He winks. "Check the bed."

"Ooh." My mood goes from negative ten to eight.

He grimaces. "Don't take this the wrong way, but we need to be out the door in like fifteen minutes."

"Okay, okay..." I jog down the hall to the bedroom and spot a dress box on the foot end. "Oh, hello." I creep up on it and pull the lid aside, revealing lush red satin... and laces. A lace-up-the-back gown? "This thing's got laces!" I shout.

"Yes, it does," says Danny from the doorway.

I hold it up. It's fancy, with a corset-like middle and a floor-length satin skirt. Looks like most of my back and shoulders will be bare. I've got a wrap that'll pair nicely with this just in case it gets chilly after dark. As fast as I can go, it still takes me about fifteen minutes to change, pretty up my hair and throw on a little makeup.

"That red really brings out your hair." Danny slides up behind me and wraps his arms around before kissing my left shoulder. "I hope it's comfortable."

"It's perfect." The dress looks like a corset, but there are no bones in it so it's nice and soft. He didn't cinch it too tight either, so I'm still able to breathe. "Thank you. It's beautiful."

We share a quick non-lipstick-smudging kiss. A wrap and heels later, we're in his BMW and back on the damnable freeway. The client, Vincent

Lennox, lives in an affluent section of LA, in a gated estate. I wouldn't call it over the top, there's no ostentatious display of wealth like some places, but it's clear the guy has cash. Enough cash for him to have hired a valet to park the car. Though, I'm guessing that man does other things for Lennox besides simply park visitors' cars.

Mr. Lennox greets us in the foyer, still walking with the help of a cane. He's a month short of fifty but outwardly appears in reasonable shape. His wife, a thin blonde with wisps of gray, rushes over and hugs Danny as though he'd resurrected Vincent from the dead. It doesn't take her long to sob into a tissue and thank him over and over again for keeping her husband out of jail. I shoot a sideways glance at Danny who winks at me. The woman's confusing lawsuits with criminal proceedings, but I don't think it would be worth splitting that hair.

Jeff Rodriguez, Danny's law firm partner, is already in the dining hall with the two paralegals, Nate Summers, an athletic man in his younger twenties with a short flat-top afro, and Hollie Andrews, who I believe is still in college but working as an intern. The girl's on the short side; she looks like an eighteen-year-old with twenty-grand of silicone in her chest. Okay, that's unfair. I guess the truth is more like twenty, five-foot-even, and movie-star pretty. And she's around Danny all day long. She's the vision of the typical blonde blue-eyed bimbo, but as soon as she opens her mouth, that goes straight out the window. She's sharp, smart, and dangerous. At least, to wives.

Nate's no slouch either, and exceedingly polite. He's totally at ease in these surroundings, in this society. I feel like the black sheep here, having grown up with hippie parents who didn't really care if any of their kids bothered with clothing before the age of ten—or if we caught a contact high from all the weed in the air. It's a bit of a culture shock for me. Heck, being a normal suburban mom feels like I've 'moved on up.' So, I sit there, with the *Jeffersons* theme rattling around in my head, mostly quiet while Danny, Jeff, and the paralegals chat about the case with Mr. Lennox.

Evidently, a prosecutor *did* sniff around at potential charges, and sat in on the lawsuit. Danny had the attending physician, who treated Mr. Lennox upon his arrival at the hospital, testify about the heart attack that rendered him unconscious. The man joked that he supposed Mr. Lennox might have studied some ancient martial art that gave him the power to self-inflict a heart attack on command so he could target the elderly couple for assassination.

Much to my delight, the legal talk only lasts for about twenty minutes and ends along with the salad course. My eyes bug out most of the night at all the fancy dishes. It feels like we're in an expensive restaurant, complete with private servers. In fact, Mr. Lennox appears to employ a small group of live-ins, judging by their familiarity with the place, who deal with the cooking and cleaning. I wonder if they do the four-course thing all the time or if this is a special occasion.

Our host becomes enamored with the paralegals, sounding a bit like a doting grandfather as he asks them about their plans. Hollie's working to become a lawyer, while Nate wants to remain a paralegal for the foreseeable future since he feels he doesn't have the right sort of personality to get up in front of a courtroom and make arguments. I tend to agree with him; he's far too nice.

The dinner is pleasant, as is the time spent in a sitting room sipping wine afterward. That's the moment Mr. Lennox is close enough to me to strike up a conversation. He's astonished I'm a federal agent and in between remarking about my looks, asks me about my work. I seem to have captivated him to an awkward degree, and I can't tell if he's feeling me out for a potential affair or if he really believes I'm as beautiful as he keeps commenting on. He's not creepy, but right as I start feeling like a unicorn he wants to stuff and mount in his gallery so he can admire it, Danny swoops in and adds himself to the conversation. Mr. Lennox pivots his attention to my husband and remarks that we're a lovely couple.

Close to ten, we exchange polite farewells and the same valet fetches Danny's BMW. As soon as my ass hits seat cushion, I kick off my high heels and let my head loll back.

"Tired?" asks Danny.

"Either that or the wine is hitting me hard. Yeah. I think I'm going to put the kids to bed and crawl in right after them."

"Mr. Lennox is an interesting guy. He never had children, so he's fascinated by young people. I think he wants to adopt my paralegals."

I chuckle. "And me. Does that mean he thinks I'm young?"

"Younger than him. For a rich guy, he's led a pretty boring life. Probably likes to get a vicarious thrill hearing about all the interesting things people do that he's too old for."

"Fifty's not ancient. He's got plenty of life left."

Danny chuckles. "Yeah, but his body's not up for it. Even before the accident. Worse now. Poor guy'll be on that cane for the rest of his life."

"That's sad." I close my eyes and drift in and out on the ride home.

***

A loud *bang* knocks me awake as the car lurches to the left. I grab on to the roof handle; tires squeal; Danny shouts, "Shit! Shit! Shit!" The BMW slides to a stop on the side of a dark, curving road by a patch of trees.

"Gunshot!" I yell, my brain on autopilot. I flick off the seatbelt, yank my duty weapon from my purse, and jump out of the car, taking cover behind the fender. I catch a fleeting shadow running off among the trees.

"Stop!" I shout. "Federal agent!" Forgetting I'm barefoot, I dart around the nose of the car and charge up the hill into the trees, hiking my dress up enough to sprint.

Grr. Why do they always run!?

The indistinct figure weaves among the trees, leaving me behind with ease. Great. I get shot at by a damn Olympic runner. It's like the laws of gravity and physics don't even apply to this dude. A rock or two underfoot cause me to stumble and curse at the pain. After a minute, I've lost the guy, so I slow to a stagger and eventual stop by a large boulder. Panting for breath, I spin around my little rocky clearing, scanning the trees for any sign of motion.

Nothing.

I'm out here in the woods at night with only a red dress to stop any bullets coming my way. Fortunately, the full moon throws off enough light for me to see. Hillcrest Park has what passes for trees around here, but they're not *that* thick. There really is something wrong with me, running out here alone like that. At a faint rustle in the underbrush behind me, I whip around, staring into the darkness, my gun up. Getting back to the car starts to feel like an awesome idea. Next, a shift in light at the corner of my eye makes me jump and swivel to the right.

I can't see anything, but I'm sure there's someone stalking me. The hairs on the back of my neck stand on end. It's impossible for anyone to be as close as the snaps and crunches in the brush suggest, yet it sounds like he's circling me so fast I can't catch sight of him while spinning in place.

And dammit, I'm completely turned around… I have no idea which way the street is, nor can I see headlights anymore.

"Damn it. I can't be *that* far from the road." I draw in a breath to shout for Danny, but a chill falls over me before I can make a sound.

The *thump-thump-thump* of rapid footfalls passes behind me. I whirl to the rear, raising my weapon, but there's no one there—only a wavering branch. A surge of wind whispers in the trees overhead while an unseen woodpecker's hammering becomes strangely loud. Since when did woodpeckers peck at night? Crickets and other bugs add in, drowning out the heartbeat thudding in my skull, and I swear the heavy rasp of a man's breathing comes from right beyond the edge of my sight.

"Sam?" calls Danny.

Oh, fuck this.

I orient on my husband's voice and take off running again. A dark, tangible presence rushes up behind me. With a yelp, I spin to my left, lashing out with an elbow at head level and bringing my Glock up again, but there's nothing there. Nothing, except for a patch of concentrated darkness among the trees about fifteen feet away, an area the moonlight refuses to touch.

And the shadow is staring at me.

That thin line between fear and terror snaps. Too terrified to scream, I bolt. Trees blur into a haze of whipping green leaves and brown smears. Danny yells again, but I can't even make out words, desperate to get away from whatever darkness is nipping at my heels. The sound of his voice pulls me onward, running until my legs burn.

"Sam?" Danny comes out of nowhere and catches me, but I'm sprinting so fast we go down in a heap, both screaming in surprise.

Gasping for breath, I scramble over him and sit up, aiming the gun back the way I came.

"Ouch." Danny stands and reaches to help me up. "Sam, what the hell is going on?"

"There's someone there," I mutter. "Took a shot at us."

Danny crouches and puts a hand on my shoulder. "No, Sam... I ran over something and the tire exploded."

I peel my gaze from the forest and stare up into his eyes. "Blowout?"

He exhales. "Yeah. Come on. Let's go home."

That was a blowout? I blink, shake my head, and don't know whether to laugh or cry. "Guess I'm on edge." I take his hand and let him pull me upright. Fortunately, the ground is dry so the dress he bought me suffered nothing a trip to the cleaners won't fix.

Danny holds me close, his hands around my waist. "You know, you running around in that dress with a gun out is the sexiest thing I've ever seen."

After a long, searching gaze at the woods—and nothing coming after me—I turn my head so we're nose to nose. "Since when are you a gun nut?"

He grins. "I'm not, but you were like straight out of a Bond movie."

My hands shake from adrenaline. I'm far too wound up to even think of feeling sexy at the moment. "Can we go back to the car?"

Danny shifts from sexy to comforting and guides me back to the car. I flop in the passenger seat, gun in my lap, and cover my face with both hands, taking slow, deliberate breaths. Ten minutes later, he tosses the jack in the trunk, gets in, and resumes driving us to Mary Lou's to pick up the kids.

"Sorry. We just raided a big gang operation with hundreds of thousands of dollars' worth of drugs. I thought it might've been retaliation."

He gives me the 'I really wish you would do something safer' grimace. "We just had a blowout. When you ran off into the park, I didn't know what had gotten into you."

"You think we should ask Mary Lou to watch the kids overnight? What if they're following us?" I twist around to look out the back window, but we're the only car on this stretch of road. I wonder if the shadow I saw was a vagrant that I just scared the shit out of. I honestly don't know what to make of the shadow… or if it was even there.

It was there, I think.

"Well, no one shot us," says Danny. "I ran over a hunk of metal. Blowouts can be loud."

I stash the gun back in my purse. "Apparently…"

My heart's still running on overdrive. I lean back and close my eyes, trying to go over what I thought I saw in my head. There's no explanation for that feeling of something predatory closing in on me, like I had seconds left to live and couldn't do a damn thing about it.

Like the beach. The beach...

Ugh. Maybe Danny's right. Could this be a stress reaction to the shooting? I've got a mandatory interview with a government head doctor later this week. Of course, if I tell them I thought a giant shadow monster chased me around the woods, I can probably kiss my career at HUD goodbye. Yeah... that's not a good idea. I think I'll chalk tonight up to a glass or two more wine than I should've had, plus nerves.

Chapter Ten
Undeclared Income

Tuesday, I'm a groggy mess. It took a long time for me to calm down enough to sleep. In the time between reliving being chased around the woods by something that didn't exist and when I finally passed out, my brain kept going back to Rosa Melendez. That entire situation bugs me like I've missed something glaring.

Three cups of coffee into my workday the next morning, I'm staring at Rosa's HUD application on my screen, and I've gone over every document I can find related to that property during the time she's lived there. On an emotional level, I'm inclined to believe her story of what happened. A woman in her situation could easily be too frightened of retaliation from a large gang with connections on both sides of the border to contact the police. Especially when she's a permanent non-citizen resident hoping to get naturalized, it would've been easy for those thugs to convince her the government would think she helped the drug operation and we'd deport her.

My brain's like a pit bull refusing to let go, but I can't find anything documented that looks out of the ordinary. I'm about to start pulling up cross references between Rosa and the gang members the FBI took into custody when Nico appears in the aisle, standing between Chad's cube and mine, *thwapping* a small blue folder against his hand.

"Moon," says Nico. "How's your side doing?"

I look up at him. "Our side is still waiting for equal pay."

He shakes his head and points at my ribs with the legal document. "Your side, smartass."

"At what level of management do they confiscate sense of humor?" I lean to my right and test my side with two fingers. "Still sore, but as long as I avoid clinging to the hood of a car during a high-speed chase, I should be fine."

He chuckles. "Good to hear. Got a present for you." He hands me the subpoena packet. "Warrant came down for your Trent case."

"Nice!" I snag it from his grip. LAPD threw us a heads up a few weeks ago. They thought the guy was dealing out of his girlfriend's place, and she was one of ours. "About time. Chad, you up for a ride?"

Chad pulls his earbuds out and leans back in his chair. "What? Did you call me?"

I wave the envelope. "Got the warrant for the

Reed house. Remember TT?"

"Oh, Tommy Trent?" Chad grins. "I remember you muttering about that."

I lock the computer and grab my jacket from the peg on the cube wall. I really look like I belong on *Law & Order* today… navy skirt suit. Don't ask me why I went there. Clothing happened before my brain recovered from sleep this morning. At least I can do the shoulder holster thing with this get up.

Nico walks backward down the aisle, still facing us. "I'll have some LAPD meet you there."

"Thanks. Can you ask them not to roll up onto the front lawn? Don't want Miss Reed flushing evidence if they beat us there." I glance at my partner. "Get moving, Heller."

Chad inhales his granola bar and slugs the last half-mug of coffee in one gulp. "Jeez Louise, I'm coming, I'm coming."

I head down the aisle in the opposite direction Nico's going, while Chad rushes into his jacket and jogs to catch up to me. Maybe wearing my Glock under my arm wasn't the best idea since it's sitting almost on top of my bruised ribs. It's irritating but not quite in the realm of painful. If there *is* some kind of divine presence responsible for creating humanity, he did a bad job. It takes us just too long to recover from injuries. Well, anyone not named the Wolverine. Lucky bastard.

Three turns, two corridors, and a door later, I emerge in the official parking lot. All our private cars go on the right side of the building. Here sits a sea of near-identical gray sedans. Ours is easy to pick out due to a darker blob on the trunk where the paint doesn't *quite* match—another repaired bullet hole. If someone had died in this car, I might feel a little strange about it, but the poor thing just got shot up.

Chad goes for the driver's side. When I hop in without my usual playful grumbles about wanting to drive, he gives me a concerned look.

"I'm okay. It's not *all* the ribs. I'm a little fried today. Not much sleep. Better you drive."

He nods and we're underway. After a few minutes on the road, he looks over. "You're pretty casual about this warrant."

I look up from reading it over. "TT's ass is still in county jail. I suppose it's possible Shante moved on already, or some of his friends came by, but the arrest report didn't mention any firearms—only industrial quantities of meth. In short, I'm not worried about getting shot up again."

Chad laughs. "Good. And it oughta be obvious if they were cooking it there."

"Doubtful, or the cops would've ripped the place apart already. I'm thinking his girlfriend was in on it, and if they distributed it out of her home—"

"Yeah, I know, Sam." He grins at me. "I do this stuff too."

"Right. Sorry. Fried."

"What kept you up so late? Kids?"

"No... had a scare last night. Danny was obligated to attend this dinner for an important client, and brought me along. On the way home, I'm dozing in and out of sleep—thinking about the shooting, and that large, organized gang… and we have a blowout."

"Oh, shit."

"Yeah. I thought someone took a potshot at us." I exhale hard. "Guess I'm a little jumpy after eating a bullet."

Chad remains quiet for a while as we sit at a red light.

"I'm fine," I say, filling in the silence. "Got an appointment with what's-his-name tomorrow. Mandatory, you know the drill."

"Good. If you ever need anything, I'll always be here to help."

"Thanks, Chad." I smile at him. "That means a lot."

His worry relaxes to a confident grin. For the remainder of the ride, we discuss the recent arrest of Thomas 'TT' Trent, a figure of no great importance. Small time drug user and dealer with a long list of priors, but nothing violent. Lots of smash and grabs, pickpocketing, B&E, possession, and so on. He's been in and out of jail since sixteen. His current status as a guest of the government would probably be shortened if he gave up his chemist's name, but as far as I know, he hasn't talked.

We're en route to the home of his (possibly ex) girlfriend, Shante Reed, the person who signed the paperwork to receive housing assistance. I more or less expect that having to wait three weeks for the warrant has reduced my chances of finding anything, but we have to at least try. There are too many honest, hardworking people in need of a helping hand to ignore when a person takes advantage of the system. The police got a bad vibe from her and sent us a request to review her case, so... here we are.

We stop in front of the house in Bell Gardens. It's a little turquoise-walled place with a dingy roof that tries to be red. An air conditioner hangs out of the window left of the front door, sealed with Hefty bags and duct tape. There's not much of a lawn to maintain; like most places around here, the grass is in a permanent state of mostly-brown.

No sooner do we get out of the car, than a local police unit rolls up behind us. Two cops walk over, a giant of an African-American on Chad's side and a youngish white guy on mine.

"Agent," says the taller man. "I'm Sergeant Wandabwa, and this is my partner, Mooney."

Chad laughs.

Mooney's face reddens. "Umm."

I narrow my eyes at my partner. If he calls me 'Moony,' there will be blood.

"Oh." Chad waves him off. "I'm not laughing at your name. Well, I am, but not for that." He thumb-points over the roof at me. "My partner, Agent Samantha Moon."

Sergeant Wandabwa grins. "There are no coincidences."

"Oh, here he goes again with that mystic crap,"

says Mooney.

"Thanks for meeting us here." I shake Mooney's hand and nod over the car at the giant, who nods back.

Chad and Wandabwa head around the nose end of our sedan and step up next to us onto the sidewalk.

"What's the deal?" asks Mooney, jabbing a thumb at the house.

I explain the warrant to search the property for evidence of undeclared income or criminal activity. "Mostly, we'd appreciate it if you watched our backs, but if you find anything incriminating, call it out."

"You got it," says Wandabwa.

I look up at him. Good grief, the guy is... the top of my head isn't even up to his shoulders.

Where were you when that kid shot me? The shooter would've taken one look at this guy and shit himself. Though the cop isn't bulging with muscles, he's just tall. *Really* tall. But that's usually enough.

Great, everyone's waiting. Guess I have lead. I open the gate in the quaint wrought-iron fence, cross the small front yard, and knock. Mooney ducks around the side of the house to watch the back. While waiting, I pull out my ID wallet, poised to hold it up.

After a few minutes of nothing, I knock again, louder.

"I ain't want no damn cookies," shouts a woman inside.

Chad bumps my arm. "You holding out on me? Save me some Thin Mints."

I smirk at him before knocking again. "Shante Reed?"

Silence hangs awkward for about ten seconds before the door opens inward, revealing a young woman about two inches shorter than me with frizzy, unruly hair. Her file lists her age as twenty-one, but she could pass for eighteen. Shante squints at the sunlight. Between her frumpy shirt and backwards shorts, I'm sure I woke her up. Great, she's some kind of vampire, sleeping in the middle of the day.

"Miss Reed." I hold up my badge. "I'm Agent Moon; this is my partner, Agent Helling. We have a warrant to search the premises."

Shante scratches her rear end, still squinting at me. "Y'all know what time it is?"

"It's 11:49 a.m.," says Chad.

"Please stand aside, miss." I offer her a copy of the warrant. "This is a copy of the warrant for your records."

She frowns at it, rolls her eyes, and wanders into the house.

It's not the messiest place I've ever had to inspect, but it would drive Mary Lou nuts—especially the miniature alien forest diorama (a plate of mold on the coffee table). The main reason our childhood home got cleaned is because my sister couldn't stand filth. Our parents were into that whole 'entropy' thing and stuff wound up where stuff wound up. And my brothers... well, little boys and mess are symbiotes. When I got old enough, I helped out... the two of us on a crusade to bring normality to hippieville.

Officer Wandabwa stays with Shante while Chad and I venture deeper into the home. Fortunately, the place is small, and it doesn't take us long to search our way to the master bedroom. I raise an eyebrow at a set of teal scrubs hanging on the back of the door. To my left, a table packed with cosmetics, brushes, and hair-care products stands on one side of the bed. The other has a long, waist-high chest of drawers, covered in junk and drug paraphernalia. That draws my attention right away, so I approach, snugging my blue latex gloves a little tighter. While I'm hardly a narcotics expert, I get the feeling this stuff has been sitting a while untouched. Miss Reed didn't *look* drug ravaged, seeming healthy, though she could play an extra in a zombie film. But then again, at 8:00 a.m. this morning, I could've said the same about myself.

"What'cha think?" asks Chad.

I peek through the drawers, finding more than a sleepover amount of men's clothes. "I think TT was living here. He's not listed in the documentation. This stuff is all his."

Chad puts his hands on his hips. "I wish we had a sniffer dog."

Conversation out in the living room between Miss Reed and Officer Wandabwa mostly involves her annoyance at being knocked out of bed early since she's due on the evening shift at the store. I glance at the scrubs. Store? I check again over her paperwork, and note that she listed her primary occupation as a part time retail sales clerk at a men's clothing place.

"Last time I checked, sales clerks don't wear medical scrubs." I point at the door.

Chad shakes his head and goes back to rummaging the surface clutter on the long cabinet.

On a whim, I check the scrubs out, going straight for the badge on the chest. It shows Shante's face but it's not a sales clerk nametag. She's also a Certified Nursing Assistant at Meadow Grove Retirement Home.

"Hey Mooney," says Chad to me.

"I know you're not going to call me that again." I give him a 'sweet' look. "What's up?"

He holds up a couple of papers, three-folded like they came out of an envelope. "She has a second job. Found a pay stub."

I nod. "Meadow Grove."

He glances at the pay stub again and tilts his head at me, bewildered. "Yeah, how'd you read that from over there? Damn, you have some sharp eyes."

I pull the ID off the scrubs and walk over, dangling the badge in front of him.

"You're good," he says.

"I'm observant. Anyway, I came here thinking she helped TT sell drugs, but I think I know why Miss Reed wasn't so sorry to see him go."

"You think she's sneaking into a care facility to

steal syringes, pills, and such?"

"Doubt it. She's really working at the home. My guess is she reports her meager retail job on her application with us, and keeps the better one quiet." I sigh. On one hand, I understand having a job where you make too much money to qualify for housing assistance but not enough to actually afford housing. From the look of that pay stub, she could probably swing a place without assistance, but it would be in a less nice area with a longer commute.

Chad shakes his head and drops the pay stub back where he found it. "Ugh."

"Now for the 'fun' part," I say.

We head back through the house toward the living room. While crossing the kitchen, a spot of white on the fridge glides by at the edge of my vision. It takes a second or two for my brain to catch up to what my eyes are telling it, and I have to step back to look again. She's got a business card pinned to the freezer door with a magnet. The card bears the word 'Marty' in sharpie marker beneath a familiar printed phone number.

"Chad…" I point at it. "Check this out."

"Huh?" He glances over.

"The raid. Rosa Melendez had the exact same card on her fridge. Tell me that's not a weird coincidence."

Chad grins, wagging his eyebrows. "There's no such thing as coincidences."

"The boy listens," says Sergeant Wandabwa, peering into the kitchen. The deep timbre of his voice reverberates off the cabinets.

We step past Officer Wandabwa into the living room where Shante Reed sits perched on the edge of the couch, her head in her hands, staring at the rug. That's a guilty look if I've ever seen one... or she's about to throw up.

"All that shit in there ain't mine. It's all Tommy's."

"So, Tommy was staying here?" I ask.

"Yeah," says Shante as a reflex. Her head snaps up to stare at me. "I mean... not *staying* here like that. He visits a lot. Or used to 'fore they picked him up. Tommy ain't dealin'. He likes weed."

"Weed? They picked him up for crystal," I say.

Shante waves her hands back and forth. "I got nothin' ta do with that crap. Weed's his, but he kept a little meth to sell."

"He get his meth from Costco?" asks Chad. "Heard they needed a truck to clear it out."

The cops chuckle.

"Miss Reed, I'm afraid there's a problem." I hold up her ID from the nursing home. "You've been receiving income that you haven't declared to HUD."

She leans back, wide-eyed, like a little girl who'd been caught stealing. Shock gives way to fear in seconds, and her hands shake. "I just got that job. Swear. Only been there a couple months. I was gonna report it, but I's 'fraid'a gettin' kicked outta here."

"Defrauding the government can be a serious

offense," says Chad, trying to sound comforting. "We don't have to go straight to prosecution. There are a number of options, including repayment of ineligible benefits."

She bows her head, crying into her hands.

The woman's upset, but I can't help but feel she's pouring it on a bit hard. "Your application at the time checked out. The violation would only encompass the period you worked for Meadow Grove without declaring that income to us. Honestly, it would've come back to us eventually via the IRS. What can you tell us about Tommy and his enterprise? Was he selling drugs out of your house?"

Shante sniffles and shakes her head. "Naw. Like I said, the boy loves his weed. That herb was all for him. The crystal he kept somewheres else."

"You abstain?" Chad asks, smiling.

"Gotta." She nods at the ID. "They do tests. My ass is strung out on account'a workin' two jobs, not no drugs. I can't lose the Grove. It's my ticket to bein' real. I didn't even—"

I tilt my head. "Go on."

She fidgets for a few seconds before looking up again. "I didn't even think it's that big a deal and all. Ain't like I'm makin' that much."

And again, I think someone's not being completely honest. "What are you leaving out?"

"I, umm, don't even know where my paperwork at. For the house and shit. I gotta hunt for it. I'll fill out whatever I gotta fill out. Please don't charge me with some fraud shit. I'll get fired, an' I'll be right back nowhere all over again."

"Should'a thought of that before committing fraud," says Officer Mooney.

Chad, Sergeant Wandabwa, and I give him the look. Really? He's one of *those.*

Shante bows her head.

"Who's Marty?" I ask.

"Huh? I ain't know no Marty."

"For a guy you don't know, why do you have his card on your fridge?" I point over my shoulder.

"Oh." She wipes her eyes. "That Marty. I ain't *know* him. He's some dude who fixes shit that breaks. Toilet plugged up, crack in the wall, that sorta business."

I pull out my notepad to jot down her employee ID number from the pay stub, as well as the address of the care home and a contact phone number. "How did you find Marty?"

"Guy came to the door and gave me the card," says Shante.

Chad pulls me aside, lowers his voice. "What's this guy do? Run down a list of HUD-managed properties or something?" He scratches his head. "Crazy odds of finding his card here, too."

"Yeah. This woman is hiding something. I'm sure of it." After I'm back in front of Shante, I say, "Are you sure there's nothing more to this Marty than a simple handyman?"

"Sure, yeah." She nods at the coffee table. "I ain't even barely call him. Tommy fix a lot of crap when he's visiting. 'Til y'all bust his ass for that weed. Why they gotta give him a hard time over a damn plant. Booze messes people's shit up way worse."

I raise a hand. "That's not a debate I'm here to make, and I think the police were more upset over the meth thing than the pot. All right, Miss Reed. Is there anything else you need to tell us? Other income, undisclosed occupants of the property, anything illegal going on here?"

She shakes her head. "Naw. Just the good job you fixin' ta take away from me."

That depends on how much she wants to keep secrets. "All right. After we finish here, I'm going to verify your employment over at Meadow Grove. We'll be back in a couple days. If your new income level alters your eligibility for benefits, the best option for you would be that we believe you didn't intend to defraud the government and made a simple mistake at not filing your paperwork. You'd be liable to repay the government for any benefits you've collected in excess of your approved amount."

"Y'all ain't gonna kick me out?" Shante stares back and forth between us. "What if I quit the boutique? Ain't makin' all that much there. Barely worth the hours I ain't sleepin'."

Chad looks around the room. "Well, turning the place into a drug den is probably not the best thing to help keep you in here. It works in your favor that TT's out of the picture. We'll need a few days to update your file. After we crunch the numbers, we'll be better able to answer those questions."

"This Marty… he have anything to do with Tommy's habit?" I ask.

Shante shakes her head. "Naw. He's just a guy to call if somethin' round the place stops workin'."

I glance at Chad. He's not leaning toward her, which tells me he's missed that she's hiding something. Or, maybe I'm starting to see shadows where there aren't any—like last night. I fish one of my business cards out and offer it to Shante. "This is my number. If you think of anything else you'd like to share with us, please call. The more cooperative you are, the better things work out for everyone involved."

Shante takes the card and holds it in her lap, staring at it. "All right."

We make another inspection pass around the place, but other than the bongs and pipes in the bedroom, nothing stands out as significant. Good for us, making the housing assistance program more honest one underemployed person at a time. Drat. I really thought going in here, I was going to unearth some major fraud that hurt truly needy people. Instead, we scared the hell out of a somewhat-needy woman. By the time we've thanked the cops for their assistance and gotten back in our car, I decide I'm not going to pursue charges here as long as she accepts a restitution agreement.

"So…?" asks Chad. "Thoughts?"

"I'm sure she's hiding something, but I don't

even know where to look."

He starts the car and pulls away from the curb. "You said the same thing about Rosa."

"Yeah."

"And she had the same 'Marty card.'" Chad shoots me a meaningful look. "Maybe they're covering for this guy. I mean, I guess it could be a simple coincidence, but it is kinda odd."

I groan and rub my eyes. "A full night's sleep has to happen before I can process this. I'm going to do a workup on Miss Reed and see how deep she's stepped in it. Part of me wants to cut her a break, but maybe if we toss around what she *might* be charged with, she'll open up that last little bit of the puzzle box."

"If you ask me, she's just freaked out by cops, and losing her house, and job. That would make anyone seem on edge. Before you hit her with the thumbscrews, I'd prefer we make sure she deserves it."

"Right. Big difference between gaming the system and making poor life choices."

"Lunch?" Chad smiles. "Super Burger?"

I laugh. "Speaking of poor life choices."

He scoffs. "Oh, come on! That place is awesome. Best fries within a fifty-mile radius."

"I know. They're not exactly the healthiest thing."

"We only go around once. You can't spend your time here stumbling through existence like a dead woman." Chad winks. "Live a little."

It *has* been a while since I had a burger, and I've been so stressed lately I'm even below my weight goal. "Ehh... Sure, why not. A little grease won't kill me."

Chapter Eleven
Six and Zero

Nick's Super Burger is one of those places that no tourist would ever dare approach.

The small coral-blue adobe restaurant covered in neon paisley looks like something that would've happened around 1900s Mexico if LSD occurred naturally in the water supply. I think it started off as this psychedelic taco stand, but that went under about ten years ago, or so I heard. Nick (at least I assume a man named Nick owns it) hasn't done much to improve the building—it's still covered with cracks, though he did get rid of the graffiti. The burger joint sits on the far left side of an otherwise open lot by a sharp bend in the road, with a scattering of metal tables and chairs out front.

Aside from it having the appearance of a dive only poor people would go near, the food is amazing. I guess the guy who runs it throws all his money at ingredients and hiring decent cooks rather than developing the property. I've always had a love/hate relationship with food. I love it, but hate what it does to my ass.

A pair of high-school kids, probably on a date, look over at us as we pull in and park. On the far left, closest to the building, sits a middle-aged woman with one of those super-wide-brimmed hats and a scarf around her head. Wow... guess she has some kind of sun allergy or something. Damn, that's gotta suck to have to wear all that stuff to go outside—especially in this heat. We pass a trio of power company men on our way to the entrance, who all stop eating to check us out, probably staring at our badges more than my boobs. Chad pulls the door open and blasts me with the smell of French fries and seared beef.

The interior is tiny, with only three small booth tables along the right side (all full of people), some coolers with drinks, and a long counter with a glass front containing all the fixings. Bins hold everything from the usual cheese, bacon, lettuce, tomato, onions, pickles, to the unusual like macaroni and cheese and even tuna salad. I stop in my tracks at that, look away, and shudder. It's my sincere hope that the tuna fish is there in case someone wants a sandwich, and not meant to go on top of a burger. A sign on the wall behind the counter announces a free meal to anyone who can finish the 'Habanero Hammer,' a half-pound monster that's about twenty percent finely chopped hot pepper. Eek. No thanks. Free food isn't worth having no sense of taste for a week.

Chad goes for a pizza burger with mozzarella and mushrooms while I'm feeling a call to a barbecue-bacon-cheeseburger. Neither of us opt for the double or triple… wholly unnecessary when the patties are an inch thick already.

It's my turn to pay, and in a couple of minutes, we're outside at one of the tables basking in the wonderful aroma of our junk food. I love how this place leaves the skin on the fries too, even if they've got enough salt to preserve a mummy. Chad dumps pepper on his fries, enough that I hold my breath until he stops to avoid sneezing.

"Jesus, Chad…" I examine the shaker, noting the contents are about a quarter-inch lower. "Enough pepper?"

"No such thing." He winks and throws a 'blackened' fry in his mouth.

This is going to be messy. I manage to cradle my burger in both hands without losing too much of the goopy cheese and barbecue sauce. The first bite is heaven on Earth. Why is it the stuff that's so horrible for us is *so* damn good?

"You stole my policy regarding garlic," I say, right before chomping down. Yeah, I kinda have a garlic addiction. Vampires beware.

Unable to laugh with a full mouth, he "mmm"s while nodding.

A few bites into my lunch, and about half my fries later, I gaze around at the other tables, squinting due to the sun. The high school kids on a date have left, but a thin guy in an expensive suit has taken their table. I say to Chad, "That card's bugging the hell out of me."

"Card?" My partner starts to take a bite, but stops. "Oh, that handyman thing?"

"Yeah."

"What about it bugs you?"

"I don't know." I bite my hamburger like it's to blame for my problems.

Chad laughs.

A few minutes of silent munching pass. These fries really are awesome.

"You could always try to find the guy," says Chad. "Check him out. If the dude does maintenance work on the cheap, it's not that surprising word would get around among people who need housing assistance."

I wag my scrap of hamburger at him. "That's just it, though. How's a guy like that make a living if he's charging so little? I'm sure it's connected to the drugs somehow."

The last of my burger dies a savage death.

Chad leans back. "Guess you *were* hungry."

Still chewing, I shrug and dust off my hands.

"Soon as we're back in the office, I'm going to dig—"

A tweaked-out metallic green Honda Accord rolls to a stop at the edge of the lot, facing to my right. The windows have too much tint to see inside, and the *lack* of loud bass music pounding out of it strikes me as suspicious. I get the unsettling feeling we're being watched.

"What?" Chad dabs at his mouth with a napkin.

Probably just some locals after a burger. Why am I so on edge lately? "Sorry. Car behind you is blinding. Anyway, I was saying… once we're back in the office, I'm going to try to dig up as much as I can on this Marty character."

The Accord's passenger side door opens, and a skinny guy in a gray hoodie hops out. I'm not sure if it's because he's got his hood up, head down, and hands stuffed in his pockets that puts me on guard, or if it's the driver wearing a bandana over his face. Probably both.

I reach under my blazer, grasping the handle of my Glock. "Trouble coming."

Chad glances back over his shoulder. The guy walks past where he should've turned left to go into the restaurant, and continues heading straight toward us. I start to pull my weapon, but before I can yell 'that's far enough,' he stops short and yanks his hand from his sweatshirt pocket. His stance sinks into a backpedal; sunlight glints from a small revolver coming up to bear on me. For an instant, I lock eyes with a Hispanic kid who can't be older than seventeen.

"Gun!" shouts Chad while leaping backward out of his chair.

My training takes over. Sinking in my chair, I sight over my weapon and squeeze the trigger.

His revolver erupts in a series of sharp *snaps*,

feeble compared to my Glock. More shots happen in front of me to the right, Chad firing from the ground. The kid keeps pulling the trigger until it clicks empty, staggering away and swooning to the side. I'm sure I hit him at least twice, but he runs back to the waiting Accord. The whole thing takes three or four seconds tops.

Chad squeezes off two more rounds at the fleeing shooter, the second causing a spurt of blood from the left knee that sends the guy flying face first into the Honda.

Hands inside pull him in while the tires smoke and squeal. I fire once more at the retreating car, but hold back for fear of a stray bullet going into one of the homes across the street. The shooter's legs fold up inside, but the door keeps flapping open. Chad sprints to the sidewalk and unloads the rest of his magazine, shattering the back window. The Accord screeches around the corner at the end of the block hard enough to make the door slam closed, and zooms off out of sight.

Everyone at the outdoor tables is on the ground, staring up at us in abject terror. The guy in the fancy suit hasn't even moved, still eating like nothing happened. I stand transfixed in the moment, my heartbeat slamming in my skull, waiting for the blinding flash of agony to tell me where I've been hit. A few seconds later, a lack of pain lets me snap out of my fog. A quick self-check finds only a splat of pizza sauce on my arm from a bullet that struck Chad's plate. His soda cup is also leaking from both sides.

Chad whips out his phone, standing on the sidewalk, suit jacket flapping in the wind. His Glock dangles from his trigger finger, the slide locked back.

"Federal agent," I say, lowering my weapon. "Everyone please stay calm and remain in the area. We'll need you to give statements."

Another more distant squelch of tires precedes a cacophony of blaring horns.

"Is anyone hurt?" I look around, mystified at my good fortune. A strip of plain steel gleams on our table where a bullet gouged away the green paint. Holy shit… that missed me by inches. About thirty feet from where I stand, blood glistens on the blacktop. Grr. How's a guy take multiple hits from a 9mm and keep on running? We need hollow points or an upgrade to .45 or something…

Patrons shake their heads and gradually pick themselves up off the ground. Since Chad's calling it in already, I holster my weapon. Faces pressed against the glass of the restaurant windows, a bunch of employees, stare at me.

Chad stuffs his phone in his pocket and walks over while ramming a fresh magazine into his Glock. "LAPDs on the way."

"That kid on something? I know I hit him at least once."

"Who knows? I'm sure I got him a couple times. They'll turn up at a hospital sooner or later. Probably dumped there by his friends who don't stick around."

"Yeah." I sigh at the blood on the ground. "Somehow, I don't think he was upset we took *his* table."

Chad grins. "You know, if you keep this shit up, your guardian angel's going to develop a drinking problem."

"Hah." I chuckle. "I don't believe in that stuff. You know that. There's no such thing as guardian angels. That kid didn't even sight over his weapon. Snub-nosed .38 at what, twenty-seven feet? It's not a mystery why he missed."

"Actually, I think that was a .32. Sounded like a cap gun." Chad pats me on the shoulder. "Still. Snubbie or not, six shots at relative close range while you were sitting down. Someone up there likes you."

I glance up at the deep blue sky and puffy white clouds. "I've been shot at twice in one month," I say. "If that's 'likes me,' I hope I never piss him off."

"Him?"

I shrug. "I figure if I have a guardian angel, it'd be a him."

"I thought you didn't believe in that stuff."

I look again at the blood on the ground. "I don't. I think."

Chapter Twelve
Dead Ends

The police show up in minutes and start collecting statements from the witnesses.

A pair of FBI agents join us soon after—since it looks like they targeted me specifically, and an attack on a federal agent makes it their show. I'm reasonably certain the kid who tried to shoot me is connected to the same gang from the raid on Rosa's house. Nick (the owner's name really *is* Nick) eagerly provides a copy of his security camera footage, which got a great view of the whole thing. Unfortunately, between the shooter's hoodie and the other two never leaving the car, it's impossible to use it for identification. The agents are unaware of any attempts on other personnel, which gets them all wondering why they came after me.

"The bushes," I say. "Those two got a real good close look at me... and dammit. This might not have been the first try."

"Not the first?" asks Special Agent Santos. "Why didn't you report it before?"

"Because I'm still not entirely sure it was." I explain the blowout and the figure in the woods—leaving out the weird feeling of being surrounded by one person who simultaneously existed and didn't. "Maybe the guy threw something into the road to kill the tire, but when he saw Danny, he chickened out."

Chad stifles a snicker.

I glance sideways at him. "What?"

"Uhh, just... erm... Danny isn't exactly the sorta guy people find intimidating."

"Yeah, yeah." I poke Chad in the side. "Still, if that was connected to this and the prospective shooter's young, seeing another person around, even Danny, might've been one thing too much for the kid's nerves. Or... we just ran something over and scared the crap out of a vagrant."

"Where'd this happen?" asks Special Agent Oakley.

"On Lemon Street by Hillcrest Park. At the elbow, a little past Lions Field," I say.

They nod and jot down notes before splitting us up. I go with Oakley to one side of the lot to give my statement of events, while Santos does the same with Chad. We also had at least six witnesses at outside tables, plus whatever the people inside managed to see out the window. Fancy suit man has a meltdown when he discovers he ate lunch while an actual gunfight occurred. He'd assumed we were shooting a movie. Must be my *Law & Order* outfit.

About two hours later, we leave the restaurant and head back to the office. I don't even bother slowing down as I approach my cube, expecting Nico will call us into his office as soon as he realizes we're back.

He's halfway out his door when we round the corner at the end of the cube row. My boss is nothing if not predictable. Once he's sure we're on our way to his office, he backs up and waits.

"Christ, you okay, Moon?" asks Nico, as soon as I walk in.

I fold my arms, pacing back and forth in a small space. "Believe it or not, I'm actually more pissed off than anything."

"That's shock talking." Nico gestures at the two chairs facing his desk. "Go on, sit down. You're probably already considering this, but I think that attack is some kind of gang retaliation for the raid the other day."

Sitting. Yeah right. I stand behind the chair, gripping the back. "That's where I was taking it too. There's something going on here with that, more than we think we see. We've found these business cards at two houses back to back, and I think this Marty—if that's even his real name—has something to do with this gang. When we were checking out Shante Reed's home, I got the strong feeling she was hiding something, but couldn't pry it out of her."

"Hmm." Nico lowers himself into his chair and leans back, rubbing his chin. "There's *something* going on, that's for sure. Rosa Melendez."

"What about her?" I ask.

Chad tilts his head.

"Miss Melendez was shot last night." Nico looks town.

I gasp. "No… What happened?"

"An unknown assailant was lying in wait outside the office building where she'd been working. She, and six other employees of her cleaning company, left the premises at 1:14 a.m. A lone individual ran up from behind and fired two shots at close range before fleeing. As far as I know, she's currently in critical condition."

My knuckles whiten on the seatback. Grr. That poor woman. As if invading her home and abusing her for over a year wasn't bad enough… "I'm going to find them."

"The FBI's gang task force is already investigating the shooting. I don't need you going off on a vendetta, especially when you seem to be on their short list too." Nico scowls at something on his monitor. "We haven't found anything that leads me to believe they're organized enough to find out who you are and be a threat to your family."

Hearing that these sons of bitches might harm my kids or Danny makes me woozy with worry and rage. I step around the chair and fall into it, holding my head. These bastards think they're hot shit, they can just kill anyone who stands up to them? It's all I can do to resist calling Mary Lou right in front of Nico to check up on her and my kids.

"We're getting close to something," says Chad. "Probably why they tried to kill Rosa. Maybe they thought she talked."

"Or would testify," I mutter.

"Could the assailant who attacked Rosa be the same guy that came after us?" asks Chad.

Nico steeples his fingers in front of his face. "Hmm. That's a possibility. From what the FBI has shared with me, these guys don't seem *too* large. Going after you two was stupid of them. They just elevated their threat level on the FBI's radar."

"That doesn't make me feel too much better." I lift my head and stare at a little gold figurine, a departmental softball trophy, on the desk until it goes blurry. "I hate not knowing."

Nico nods. "Well, then find out. If Rosa wakes up, she may be more inclined to talk."

I nod, following his train of thought. "They already tried to kill her. Keeping quiet isn't going to help her."

"Assuming she wakes up," says Chad, ever the optimist.

I bow my head. "If there *is* such a thing as guardian angels, mine needs to give Rosa's a slap upside the head."

Nico chuckles. "Six shots at close range and you walk away without a scratch. Pretty impressive. Go buy a lottery ticket. Oh, that reminds me... Dr. Weir is expecting you tomorrow at ten."

"Gonna get your head shrunk," says Chad with a wink.

"She's meeting *you* at eleven thirty." Nico smiles at him.

Chad's grin shifts flat. "I'm fine."

"It's routine procedure for agents involved in shootings. Look on the bright side. You two had a second fire incident before you made it to your psych appointment for the first. Might as well do a two-for-one special." Nico's soft chuckle morphs into a concerned expression. "I'm glad you two are okay. Tactical Kevlar would intimidate anyone you need to interview, of course, but you might want to consider at least a vest under your street clothes for the time being."

"Thanks, and yeah… not a bad idea." I stand. "I have a Marty to catch."

Nico raises an eyebrow. I explain the cards we found at Rosa's place as well as Shante's, and how both women gave me almost the exact same response when I asked who he was, as if they'd been coached. He raises his arm and gives us his 'go forth and discover' gesture of dismissal.

I return to my cube by way of the bathroom. At least by the time I'm done in there, my hands have stopped shaking. As soon as my ass hits my desk chair, I dial Mary Lou.

"Sam? What's up?"

"Just checking in, making sure everything's fine."

"Billy Joe, stop that!" shouts Mary Lou in the

background before coming back on the line. "Oh, everything's peachy. Nothing I can't handle. I don't know what you did with Tammy, but she's so sweet. Wish I could get *my* four-year-old to behave that well."

I grin. "Luck of the draw. Anthony's not giving you any trouble?"

"Well, he got into a fight with Ruby Grace over the potty. He used it, she thinks it's hers, screaming happened. Now she won't go near it because it's got 'boy germs.'"

"Heh. Tell her she can cover his with girl germs soon. Hey, keep an eye out, okay?"

"Oh, shit. What's wrong?" asks Mary Lou in a half-whisper.

"I… I'm being overly cautious." I can't say a drug gang is literally gunning for me or she'll lose her mind. "Saw an alert of a number of burglaries in your area. Guy's still out there. All I'm saying is keep an eye open."

"Aw, shit. All right. This guy dangerous?"

"Probably."

Mary Lou whines out her nose. "Geez, Sam. You go on—and tell me whenever they catch the guy, all right? I ain't gonna be able to sleep now, but thanks for warning me."

"I had to." I smile a guilty smile to myself.

We chat for a few minutes more about the kids and Ricky. She's still worried he might be cheating on her, but hasn't had the courage yet to ask him about it. Though, he also hasn't gone out with the guys after work again, so maybe he really did as he said. She thinks he's been anxious lately, which I suggest might be job related. While I'm encouraging her to talk to him, Ellie Mae screams, "Mom!" seconds before something crashes to the floor and another kid starts wailing.

"Gotta go," says Mary Lou. "Billy Joe just pulled a shelf down on top of himself."

"Oh, no! Is he okay?" I bite my finger. "Sorry for distracting you."

"I think he's more scared than hurt. Let me get going."

"Okay."

After we hang up, I stare at my computer, overwhelmed by the need to do whatever I have to do to keep my family safe. My brain's going in spirals of worst-case scenarios and what I could possibly come up with to make sure none of them ever happen. If I have to track this 'Marty' back to Tijuana myself, so be it. None of my searches on home contractors or small 'handyman' companies give me anything promising. I run the number on the card and it comes back as being a residential number assigned to Newvox, a VOIP telephone service. That's not too unexpected... a lot of small one-person businesses use the voice-over-internet phones because they're cheap. Another potential red flag is that these lines aren't married to a physical location. They can be even more phantom than a prepaid cell phone.

Another database search links the telephone

number to a Mr. Haresh Kondapalli. A little poking around on the Newvox website tells me their primary focus is customers who use the service to make cheap international calls. Could be that the guy took 'Marty' as a generic name that people could remember more easily.

Test one. I dial out on our phone system in a way that presents a fake caller ID and name. If someone calls it back within about twenty minutes, it'll transfer it to my desk, but the person I call won't know the government's sniffing around. Comes in handy sometimes when we don't want to tip off suspects that they're being investigated.

"Hey, you got Marty. What can I help you with?" says a rather energetic—and not-very-Indian-sounding man.

"Hi. A woman I work with gave me this number. She said you fix things around the house and don't charge too much?"

"Ahh, yeah," says Marty. "Have I been to your place before?"

"No. My water heater is on the blink and I need someone to take a look at it."

"Hmm. Let me check my… oh. Looks like I'm pretty solid booked for at least two months. I can pencil you in for… say, September 18th?"

He's clearly not interested, which sets off a red flag. I'm sure this line isn't really used for request-ing home repairs. "Oh, I really needed something faster than that. Sorry. I guess I'll try to find another repairman."

"I understand. Sorry I couldn't be of more help. I got more work than I can handle." He chuckles, eerily friendly and honest sounding. A little too much so, like a snake oil salesman. "You have a good day, awrite?"

"Thanks, I'll try." I hang up.

Something tells me I did *not* just speak to Mr. Haresh Kondapalli.

I dial out again, this time using a normal line with the official Caller ID information, and call Newvox. Trying to skip their IVR menu by mashing 0 dumps me to a customer service queue and hold music so awful I think it should legally count as torture. Ugh.

"You okay?" asks Chad from across the aisle.

"Did you know that my call is very important?" I ask. "And that my estimated wait time is two minutes?"

Chad laughs. "Your computer broke or something?"

"Nope. Tracking down a lead."

"Hello, and thank you for calling Newvox. My name is"—the woman mumbles something indecipherable but foreign sounding—"may I have your name and account number please?"

"Hi. I'm Agent Samantha Moon with the Federal Department of Housing and Urban Development. I need to speak to someone in your legal department, or to someone who can help me with the details of one of your customers' accounts pursuant to an active investigation."

"Do you have an account number?"

"I've got the phone number."

"All right," says Indecipherable. "May I please have the phone number?"

I give her the number from Marty's card.

"Would you please confirm the security phrase for the account?" asks the woman.

Ugh. I lean back and stare at the drop ceiling panels. "I don't think you can help me, Rita"—closest thing I can come up with to what her name sounded like—"I'm calling from the federal government regarding an ongoing investigation."

"I'm sorry, miss. I cannot open the account without the correct answer to the security question. It is for your own protection and security. I can answer your general questions about Newvox."

The pits and holes in the drop ceiling tile grow larger, like I'm falling upward in slow motion. "Can I please speak to your supervisor?"

"Hold on one moment."

Awful music pummels my ears, the same eight notes looping. Four minutes later, a man with a similar accent comes on the line. "Hello. I am Srinivas, supervisor of Priya. How may I help you?"

I repeat my explanation while making zombie faces at the ceiling. This guy at least seems to be capable of actual communication and not simply reading from an index card of prefab responses. Wow, maybe I *did* actually get a supervisor and not the guy in the next cubicle. He transfers me again, and after eight minutes on hold, a woman with a southern accent picks up.

"Hello? Newvox, this is Ruth Ann."

Hmm. Wonder if she knows my sister? Maybe there's a double name club or something.

"Hi…" I say, more a sigh than speech. "I hope you can help me…" I repeat my explanation for the third time. Ruth Ann apparently works in some 'advanced customer service' capacity and can't release their customer's account information to a third party. Argh. However, she does transfer me to Newvox's legal department where I get a wonderfully polite man named Corey on the line. I identify myself again, give him my badge number, and he agrees to help.

"Agent Moon, the number you gave me appears to be a secondary line on this account. I'm going back three years and it doesn't appear to have ever made an outbound call. However, looks like they've got it set up to forward all incoming calls instantly to another number."

"Can you give me that number? And the address to which the account is registered?"

"Of course." He reads it off slow, and I jot it down. It's local at least, judging by area code. The address is reasonably close as well, in Omaha Heights, a little northeast of LA. "Anything else I can help you with, Agent Moon?"

"Yes, actually. Would you be able to fax me or email me a list of inbound telephone numbers who've called the VOIP line?"

"I can, but for that, we'd need something

official in writing."

"Sure. That's not a problem. Where can I fax you the warrant?"

Corey reads me off a number, which I also jot down.

"Thanks Corey. Please tell me you have a direct line I can get you back on if I need to?"

"I do." He gives me a number and an email address. I'm nearly giddy. "I'm going to go submit the warrant request now. You'll probably have a fax within a couple days."

"Great. I'll keep my eye out for it," says Corey.

We hang up. I slouch back in my chair, in dire want of coffee. "Well, that was only severely painful."

Chad leans into my cube, offering me a Styrofoam cup. "Black as you like. Dunno how you can tolerate it."

"You're a mind reader." I grab the coffee, sniff it, and let off a sigh of adoration. Fresh, too. The man is a saint.

"Hardly. I merely observed the way you were attempting to burn the ceiling with your eyes." He grins, sips his coffee and returns to his cube.

After sending my request to Nico regarding the warrant for the call activity, I plug the forwarding number into the system. Unsurprisingly, it comes back as a prepaid phone.

"Hah!" I pound my fist into the desk. "I knew it!"

Chad rolls back in his chair, staring at me past

his cube wall, his coffee cup pressed to his lips.

"Marty's part of this. Fake number forwarding to a burner phone." I wave the paper with Haresh Kondapalli's address on it at him. "We're hitting the road…. After we get vests."

Chapter Thirteen
Wild Geese

The address Corey from Newvox gave me comes up in our database as a HUD-managed property, though the file hasn't been updated in three years.

Nothing red-flags in the computer, and the tenant's name is even Haresh Kondapalli. Finally, something that lines up. It's odd that no one updated the record, but when you're understaffed, under-appreciated, and our budget is always under attack by conservatives, something getting overlooked here hardly surprises me.

I love my job, but is it a bad sign I'm showing early-onset cynicism?

After printing the file, I toss it in a manila folder and follow Chad outside. I feel like driving time, so I walk a little faster than him (not difficult since he's still nursing coffee) and hop in behind the wheel. He doesn't react, taking the passenger seat without a word.

On the ride to Omaha Heights, I bounce what I've found so far off him.

"That *is* strange," says Chad. "Why would a maintenance guy need a throwaway phone?"

"My point exactly." I pull into the left lane in anticipation of a turn, and stop at a red light. "I'm hoping Haresh can help us out with that part. I sent a warrant request up the pipe for the inbound call records."

"Think you'll get it?"

I shrug as the light changes green. "I don't see why not. Organized drug activity occurred at a property where we found that card, and a witness has been shot. The redirection on that phone number is highly suspicious. Maybe I can find some pattern with the numbers."

"Or you'll wind up having to hand it off to the FBI."

A guy on a mountain bike nearly gives me a heart attack when he comes out of nowhere, flying in front of me as I turn. I jam on the brakes, missing the bike by inches. The guy looks back at me and has the balls to flip *me* the bird. Chad goes off, hanging out his window and giving the guy a master class in profanity. The cyclist keeps waving his middle finger at us, not looking where he's going. I'm a half second from throwing the car into reverse and going after him, not that I have any authority over traffic laws, but before I do, the cyclist plows face-first into a street sign post and wipes out.

So that's what instant karma looks like.

Screw it. With Chad still shouting at the guy about where he's going to wind up wearing his little bike helmet, I step on the gas... and the idiot behind me decides I took too long, so he rides my ass. Easy fix for that... I flick on the emergency lights for a few seconds, which makes him back off. Let him think we're undercover PD, assuming he doesn't notice the federal license plates. Ugh. It almost feels like fate is telling me not to do this. Or maybe I'm moody and uncomfortable due to the bulletproof vest I put on under my shirt. It's smaller and thinner than the tactical armor I wore at the raid, but it's almost undetectable. Granted, if someone shoots me again, I'll have *broken* ribs instead of bruised ones—but that beats a punctured vital organ.

No other irritations plague me on the rest of the trip. At least until I pull up in front of Haresh Kondapalli's house and spot a pair of little girls running around the front yard in bathing suits, jumping over a lawn sprinkler. They appear to be about eight, and identical twins, utterly adorable blonde, blue-eyed angels. I'm no geneticist, but I don't think Mr. Kondapalli is their dad.

The front door is open, and the flicker of an active television paints the plain white wall inside.

"What?" asks Chad, still wiping at his leg with napkins. "What are you staring at?"

"Unless Mr. Kondapalli has a young daughter who invited two friends over to play, I think I'm about to get frustrated."

Chad leans closer to peer past me out the driver's side window. "Cute kids. Why would they frustrate you?"

"Would you guess their last name is Konda-palli?"

"Oh." Chad sits up straight. "Good point."

I open the door and stand out of the car. The girls stop running about, watching me with curious expressions. When I approach the gate in their chain-link fence, the one nearer the house yells, "Mom, someone's here."

A blonde woman in her late thirties appears in the open doorway, wearing a pink half-tee and gym shorts. She's as skinny as the kids and quite tan, gotta be a sun-worshipper. Who else in California leaves the AC *off* in July?

The kids resume playing with the water sprinkler, mostly ignoring us as we approach the porch.

"Who are you?" asks the woman, a hitch of nervousness in her voice.

"Good afternoon, ma'am." I hold up my ID and introduce Chad and myself. "I'm following up on an investigation. We're looking for a man named Haresh Kondapalli."

She makes a bewildered face and shrugs. "I don't know anyone by that name. Why are you even asking me that?"

Chad clasps his hands in front of himself, his eyes locked on the woman's feet. Her outfit doesn't leave a whole lot to the imagination, so he's trying not to be creepy.

I open the manila and check the documents. "This is 4502 Cato Street?"

"Yes."

"Are we in trouble?" asks one of the kids.

I smile at them. "No, sweetie. I'm just trying to fix some old records. No one's in trouble."

The girls grin at me and continue playing in the water.

"How long have you lived here, miss…?"

"Angie McCoy." She looks up and to the side, biting her lip. Not a lie, but she's probably not good at remembering specific dates. "Been a couple years now."

"Would it be all right if we had a look around inside?"

She scrunches up her face. "Why would you need to do that?"

"This house is managed through HUD, which means we can perform inspections."

"Oh." Angie shakes her head. "You guys gotta update your system. We're not receiving any kind of assistance. My husband and I bought this place on a foreclosure sale, 'while back. Maybe the people who used to live here were on that HUD thing, but we aren't."

"Do you have a gun?" asks a childish voice to my left.

Both kids are standing by Chad, gazing up at him like Thor himself came to visit. Or at least

Thor's brunette brother.

"Looks like you've got a fan club," I mutter.

Chad side-eyes me for an instant before smiling at the kids. "Federal agents are armed, yes."

The girls take a step a back, though they still look awestruck.

"Hang on a sec?" asks Angie, before padding into the house. "I'ma call Chris and see if he remembers."

My nerves prickle, for all I know, she's going inside to grab a gun... but I have to hope she's not going to do anything that stupid with two small girls here. Speaking of which, they continue to pepper Chad with question after question. At least he's comfortable around children. If HUD doesn't work out for him, he could get work as a mall Santa.

Angie wanders back into view with a cell phone against her head, muttering, "Uh huh," over and over. After a few repetitions, she looks up at me. "Chris said he thinks the guy that used to live here was that Pally something. Place got foreclosed on or some such thing, and we got it at a cheap auction."

Feels like she's being straightforward. Grr. That should've been documented in our system, especially if someone receiving partial assistance defaulted on the payments. Oh, *please* be ineptitude and not complicity. "Have you ever heard of anyone named Marty?"

"Umm. I had a friend in high school named Marty. Chris works with someone named Marty, and I think the real estate guy was named Martin.

That counts as a 'Marty' right?"

"Yeah." I feel like slapping myself in the forehead, but I stay professional. "Thank you for your time. That's all I needed."

Angie nods. "Do you need any kinda documents about the mortgage?"

"Thanks, but I can verify that from the office." Which I probably ought to have done before driving out here. "No need to bother you any more than we already have."

"All right. Have a nice day."

"You too. Sorry for bothering you." My smile is only somewhat plastic, and as soon as I'm plodding back to the car and these people can't see my face, I scowl.

Chad strolls beside me, making an exaggerated show of looking all around.

"You see something? What are you looking for?" I ask, my hand edging toward my sidearm.

He grins. "Wild geese. Or maybe just a goose."

I glare at the clouds, shake my head.

When we reach the car, Chad shields his hand over his eyes, searching left and right. I pick my eye with my middle finger, which makes him laugh and get in. The second my fingers touch the door handle, my cell phone rings. I pull the door open anyway, and stand in the space between it and the car while answering.

"Hello?"

"Sam?" asks Mary Lou, sounding worried. "You got a minute?"

"Sure." I sink into the car and sit. "Is something wrong?"

"Last night… I thought I saw someone prowling around the house. Ricky went outside to check. He didn't see anyone, but the weirdest thing happened."

I rub the bridge of my nose, my mood slam-shifting from frustration to anger in an instant. If those gang bastards go near my sister… "Weird how?"

"Well, like right before I spotted the guy, Ruby Grace just starts screaming outta nowhere. Like somethin' scared the devil outta her. When I'm running down the hall to her room, I get hit with this overpowering feeling of fear. Like someone's standing right behind me, about to stab me. I couldn't move for a sec, but I screamed and ran back to our room ta wake Ricky. He went on and checked, and Ruby Grace was fine, just a li'l ol' nightmare."

My mind jumps back to how I felt in the woods, that ponderous feeling of impending doom, as if death itself hung on my shoulders. It's too bizarre to even contemplate, so I push it aside. "You said Ricky didn't find anyone?"

"No, Sam. No tracks, nothin' outta place. He thinks I had one of those uhh, 'waking nightmare' things. Told me to forget it, but I keep thinking about Ruby Grace. If I had a nightmare, why was she screaming?"

"She okay?" I ask.

"Yes. Everyone's fine. I..." Mary Lou lets out a long sigh. "S'pose I'm just bein' hormonal or something."

"It's all right." My boss didn't seem to think this gang had the resources to figure out exactly who I am and target my family, but still, I'm not ready to dismiss that so easily. "Well, that burglar I mentioned hasn't been caught yet. Keep alert, and make sure your doors are locked."

"I will. Oh, I guess you're still at work now, huh."

"Yep. How're Tammy and Anthony doing?"

"Oh, perfect. Got 'em all plopped down watchin' Disney." Mary Lou chuckles.

"You're a lifesaver. Thank you for watching them so much."

"Aww, it's nothing. Least I can do since I don't gotta work. See you in a couple hours."

"You bet. Later."

Chad raises an eyebrow. "Bad news?"

"I don't know. I think my sister just had a bad nightmare last night and needed to talk about it."

He grins. "Good. You want me to drive back or did you need to run over another bike to beat your high score?"

I smirk and slam my door a little too hard. "One bike wouldn't do it. I need two, plus a crossing guard."

Chad laughs.

The whole ride back to the office, I grumble to myself about this investigation going in circles. No armor is perfect. No liars are without vulnerability. All I need to do is to find the crack.

And wedge it wide open.

Chapter Fourteen
Hunting Phantoms

We arrive back at the office a touch past four in the afternoon. I can leave at five, but my urge to uncover who this Marty guy is clashing with my need to have my children close. Despite Nico's opinion, something doesn't feel right to me. Maybe it's merely my frustration at this investigation. So far, I've had about as much luck as trying to crack open a coconut with a toy plastic sword.

"Moon, Helling," says Nico from the end of our row, leaning to the right in preparation to walk back to his office. "Got a minute?"

Dammit. Now what? Our boss vanishes around the cube wall as soon as I nod, and by the time I reach his office, he's already sitting behind his desk. Chad follows me in, and we sit in the two facing chairs.

"Good news this time." Nico smiles. "The

shooter from Super Burger turned up in LA Community Hospital, along with two buddies. Evidently, they initially claimed to be victims of an unprovoked gang shooting, but the LAPD traced one of them to a beetle-green Accord that matched your description. They're running ballistics now on slugs recovered from the car and the suspects. I expect they'll match your weapons."

I slump with relief. "Finally, some good news."

"Wow. They're all alive?" Chad blinks.

"That's what the police are saying." Nico grins. "Though, one is in pretty rough shape. Even better, the FBI has been all over this. The gang's quite a bit smaller than we initially thought. They picked up another four individuals with connections to the three amigos in the Accord. You can probably stop looking over your shoulder now."

Lucky… for both of us. I chose HUD because I thought it offered the best opportunity to be a federal agent with the least chance of winding up in a life-or-death situation. And here I've had two inside of two weeks. Though, with the last remnants of that gang in custody, maybe I can finally breathe easy about someone trying to hurt Mary Lou or my kids.

"My sister called me earlier and said someone had been prowling around her house last night. Think you could get the FPD to keep an eye on the place for a couple days 'til we get this gang sorted out?"

Nico looks sympathetic, but shakes his head.

"Do you have anything more concrete than you think they *might* go after her? Did she get a good look at the guy?"

I sigh. "No. She just saw a shadow move and got spooked."

"Damn." Nico cringes. "I'm sorry, Sam, but I'd need more than that. The police are going to want something concrete before they throw budget at security detail. I hate to make it sound so mercenary, but there are only so many cops."

"I understand." I do, but understanding and gracefully accepting aren't the same thing. "When do you want us to go ID the shooter? I got a brief look at the kid with the gun, but the driver had a bandana over his face, and the third guy must've been in the back seat. I didn't see him at all."

"Same here," says Chad. "I can peg the shooter, but never saw the other two. They didn't get out of the car."

"Right." Nico taps a pen on the fingers of the left hand. The repetitive *click-click-click* gets annoying fast. "Probably a few days, though if the ballistics match, your not getting a look at the other two won't matter that much. If anything changes, I'll let you know. Do you have anything for me?"

"Not yet." I give him an overview of the Marty situation and the VOIP line. "Kondapalli's house turned out to be a dead end. There's a woman living there now who claims the house was sold at auction, but our system's got nothing about it."

Nico groans. "Let me guess, roughly three years

ago?"

I nod.

"One name. Donnie Vento. He left a swath of grade-A shit through our system in the short year he worked for us. Montoya's good, but it's quite possible he missed one of the cases Donnie twisted up. Took him six months to un-fuck everything. Say the name 'Donnie Vento' to anyone who's been here four years or more, and they'll probably throw heavy objects at you."

Chad blinks. "Guy half-asses it that bad and he lasts a whole year?"

"Oh, he worked just hard enough to bury his trail. He was clever, and didn't overdo it so much that his case resolve rate stood out as too good. Out of every five cases he pulled, he just closed three as fixed without doing anything. Anyway, ancient history." Nico gestures at me. "Uhh, Moon, would you mind fixing that case record since you've already got your hand on it?"

"Sure."

I tromp back to my desk, hiding my anger in all ways but for how hard my feet hit the carpet. Between not being able to get a police detail on my sister's place and having an old mess dumped in my lap fifteen minutes before I can walk out the door, I'm ready to bite someone's head clear off. It's not Nico's fault. The guy who half-assed it originally was fired before I ever got here. Not like I can make him fix it.

Back at my cube, I send a text to Danny, asking

him to pick up the kids from Mary Lou's since I'm going to be late. That done, I dive into the computer system and go on a hunt. By 5:08 p.m., I've found a record of the foreclosure sale. Chris McCoy and his wife Angie are listed as the current owners, and they're not on any program with us. HUD kept sending assistance payments after Kondapalli no longer lived there, but they only represented about forty percent of the monthly mortgage. In fact, we're *still* sending them. Ugh. I already want to shove Vento's head in a toilet and flush it a few times. Calling the bank now would be pointless since no one who works in any capacity to address this is going to be there at this hour. I'm going to have to get someone on the phone, hope the bank has been keeping this money in some kind of escrow, and have them send it back to HUD. Stopping future payments though, that I can do.

I'm finished with cleaning that record up at 5:42 p.m., and since I'm already late, I run the name 'Haresh Kondapalli.' It comes back with over a hundred hits. Ugh. Screw this.

"Wow. That's a lot of entries," says Chad, leaning on the entrance to my cube. He's got his coat draped over his back on two fingers, ready to get out of here. "You sure you're not wasting time?"

"Maybe, but I got a feeling there's something here… and I'm going to find it." I stand and lock my workstation. "Just not tonight."

Chad laughs. "Hey, well at least they got that

jackass from Nick's."

"At least there's that." I snug my coat on and grab my purse. "You dig up anything else on Rosa's house?"

He shakes his head. "Not really. Saw an email about the DEA recovering enough product in there that Villero's looking at so much time they're going to keep his cremated remains in Leavenworth for a few decades after he's gone."

"Heh. Thanks. I needed to smile."

And now, I need to get home to my family.

Chapter Fifteen
Family Tradition

The powerful fragrance of spaghetti sauce saturates the house when I walk in the door. Tammy springs off the sofa and darts across the living room, leaping into my arms.

"Mommy's home!" she shouts.

Anthony rolls over onto his chest and slides feet first off the sofa before wobbling up to me. "Hi, Mommy. Late."

I toss my purse onto the coffee table and pick him up with my free arm. "I know, hon."

"Did you catch the bad guy?" asks Tammy.

"I'm working on it." I kiss them both on the head... then do it again.

Danny peeks in from the kitchen archway. "Everything okay at work?"

"I had to clean up a mess."

Anthony shakes his head. "I didn't do it!"

I squeeze him, nearly laughing myself to tears. It's good to be home. "No, but you'd probably have made a better agent than the guy who made the mess."

"I can be agent." Anthony nods.

"No, you can't," says Tammy. "You're two. Agent's gotta be really old, like Mom."

I smirk.

Danny stifles a snicker and ducks back into the kitchen. "Dinner's ready."

After carrying the kids into the kitchen and putting them down, I hug Danny while he's trying to transfer a large pot of sauce from the stove to the table. "Give me a moment to change," I say.

"Sure thing, babe." He kisses me quick and sets the pot down on a thick cutting board.

I head to the bedroom and trade my skirt suit, hose, and shoes for a t-shirt and sweat pants since my husband is a big fan of air conditioning. We could store meat in our hallway. By the time I get back to the kitchen, Anthony's eating and Danny's slicing a sausage for Tammy. Usually, he makes this sauce with hot Italian sausage, but since we had the kids, he always throws in a couple non-spicy ones for them.

My body melts into the chair and, despite being famished, I can't find the energy right away to eat. Instead, I sit there watching Danny sectioning sausage into little discs, and simply grin. Tammy's got an expression like a scientist working out the last few equations to make the Manhattan Project work, but she's experimenting with that whole twisting-pasta-onto-a-fork thing.

Maybe I'm reaching my wits' end with a frustrating case, I almost got killed twice in two weeks, and there's probably a street gang out there still after me, but at this moment, I feel like the luckiest woman in the world.

Without Danny, I don't know where I'd be or what I'd do with myself. Watching him make up some silly story about the Pasta King and his sausage farms for Tammy is so damn cute I wind up crying silently into my napkin. It's mostly the stress of the past two weeks, but this fleeting moment is about as perfect as life can be.

He takes his seat, sending an 'are you okay' stare over the table at me. When I grin, he does too, and we eat while Tammy tells me all about her day. About halfway through dinner, she hits me with a low blow.

"I wish you could be home all day like Aunt Mary Lou."

I lean over and ruffle her hair. "Me too, Tam Tam."

Her hazel eyes widen with earnest innocence. "Do you have to work 'cause Daddy doesn't make as much money as Uncle Ricky?"

Danny coughs.

"Uncle Ricky's been doing that job for a really long time," I say. "Your father's just started his own office. It takes a while for it to pick up."

"Oh." Tammy thinks that over for a moment.

"Daddy should be a 'lectric man like Uncle Ricky an' not a lawyer."

Said no mother ever. "There's nothing wrong with being an 'electric man' or a lawyer."

"If I play my cards right, maybe in a year or two, Mommy won't need to work anymore." Danny winks at me.

Being able to stay home with the kids all day would be like a dream come true… at least when they're little. Eventually, they'd get tired of having me over their shoulder constantly. I chuckle, and lose myself in Danny's spaghetti sauce. He's ruined me for Italian food, since we have yet to find a place with sauce comparable to his.

After dinner, we squeak in a little more than two hours of family time, huddled together on the sofa watching a cartoon movie, *Ice Age*. Damn. Marty is the acorn and I feel like that poor squirrel-thing. Danny and I connect on an unconscious level and wind up letting the kids stay up about forty minutes late to make up for when I got home. They don't seem to notice bedtime slip by, but once they start keeling over, we carry them down the hall. Anthony must've been as wild at Mary Lou's as Tammy said, since he passes out before Danny's even finished putting pajamas on him. Eventually, teeth are brushed, stuffed animals are clutched, foreheads are kissed, and lights go out.

Danny starts heading back to the living room, but I snag his arm and drag him three steps to our room.

"This is a relax in bed night."

He kisses me. "All right. I'll catch up in a few minutes... dishes."

"You're amazing."

He leans back and strikes a pose that says 'yes, I know,' but only holds it for a second before a sincere smile replaces the cockiness. "So are you. It's tight now, but there's a light at the end of the tunnel. A couple of judgments go my way, word goes around, more clients... we'll be set."

"Sounds like a plan," I say.

Of course, I'll probably stay on with HUD. The money is only part of it. I didn't spend years working my ass off to get in the door there only to walk away.

While he goes off to clean up the kitchen, I change into a nightgown and sprawl on the bed. It's so damn soft I'm tempted to surrender to sleep right away. Twenty or so blessed minutes of comfort later, Danny walks in. I scoot back to sit up against the headboard while he undresses to his boxer briefs and climbs in next to me under the covers.

We lean against each other and grumble about how stressful our respective days were. Danny's worries about the law firm sound like he's focusing on his partner Jeff's 'flakiness,' but I'm sure he's mostly upset that he's still not making as much as I do. While I don't believe he'd ever actively resent me for that, his personality and upbringing don't sit well with a woman out-earning him. Danny's mother is one of those people who still believes women don't belong in the workforce. Of course, if his law firm *does* take off, he stands to make insane amounts of money.

Eventually, I'm half-watching the little TV past the foot of the bed and he's somewhat engrossed in a novel—*The Da Vinci Code*.

"Thanks for making dinner. I really, really, *really* love your sauce." I smile to myself, and swish my feet side to side. "When I'm a little old lady, I'll *still* crave it."

Danny grasps my hand. "Mama made sure I knew how to make it before I moved out to college. You know, the whole 'shunned by my ancestors' thing if I couldn't get it right."

I shift my weight and lean against him, my head on his shoulder. "Are you going to teach the kids how to make it?"

"Not if Mama's still around when they want to learn. She's a much better instructor." Danny kisses the top of my head.

It's so easy to close my eyes. "I'll not be having your mother threatening our children with ancestral doom over lackluster tomato sauce."

He laughs. "You know, we should really visit my parents at some point soon. They haven't seen Anthony since he was an infant."

"Sure. As soon as life gets sane."

"Hey." Danny pokes me in the side. "If you never want to see them again, they'll be crushed."

As if. Despite my degree and being a federal agent, I'm still 'that hippie girl' who's not good enough for their precious little Daniel. Also, my not believing in the whole religion thing is a major issue. Icicles practically form on the walls when I'm in the same room with his mother. His father's not *quite* as bad. After an hour of talking to me, he realized I'm not like my parents, but he still thinks I'm going to Hell.

I say, "I didn't mean *actually* sane. I meant as soon as I don't have a hot mess of an investigation on my plate." For Danny's sake, I can tolerate an afternoon of torment… eventually.

He strokes my hair. "Is that why you look so exhausted?"

"Yeah. I spent half the day trying to find a man who doesn't seem to have existed." I ramble on about the forwarded phone, the prepaid cell, and this 'Marty' guy. "That phone account's probably set up with a fake name. Tomorrow, I get to spend hours going through data, and I still don't even know exactly what I'm investigating."

Danny chuckles. "How'd you wind up investigating if you don't even know what it is?"

"Two HUD properties, both had drug use going on there, both had a business card for a guy supposedly named Marty who's trying to hide himself. That's not something a legitimate handyman does."

One thing about Danny's air conditioning fetish, it makes snuggling in bed awesome.

"Sounds like he's probably a big-time dealer. They call that number when they need a delivery."

I yawn. "That would explain why everyone's got the same story when I ask who he is."

"Leave the drug stuff to the FBI or the LAPD, and stop driving yourself crazy."

"Maybe... I might just wind up frustrated to the point I don't have a choice. Oh... there's something else."

He stops stroking my hair. "What? That's a scary tone in your voice."

I sit up straight, let out a deep breath, and tell him about the shooting at the burger joint.

"Jesus effing Christ, Sam." Danny grabs me by the shoulders. "You sat on that the whole time you've been home? You could've been killed!"

I half smile. "You just took God's name in vain. Your mother's head would spin all the way around."

"Sam. I'm serious." He lets his head sag. "Why didn't you tell me right away?"

"Sorry. I didn't want to talk about that in front of the kids, and you're right when you said I'm exhausted. My brain is already half shut down for the day."

Danny wraps his arms around me and sniffles into my shoulder. "Please don't make me have to deal with losing you. Can't you do something safer?"

Here we go again. I don't have the energy for this now. "HUD *is* safe. By comparison anyway. It's an anomaly. I could work for them for the next forty years and never wind up even needing to touch my gun again. Look, can we maybe talk about this later when I'm not ready to pass out?"

"Okay." He holds me for a moment more, sighs, and leans back against the headboard, the novel in his lap. "I'm worried about you."

I squeeze his hand. "It's okay. I got a guardian angel... or so Chad tells me."

"Now I *know* you're tired." Danny gives me a sad smile. "You don't believe in that stuff."

Tammy lets off a horrible, loud shriek of terror, then shouts, "Mommy!"

When did she start having nightmares? I fling the covers off and slide out of bed. "I got it."

The hallway outside the bedroom feels darker than it ought to be, and a hanging cloud of shadow blocks my view of the living room. Shifting and swaying, the walls seem to drift farther away and glide back in a disorienting dance. Paralytic fear wells up out of nowhere, the same unnatural dread that seized me in Hillcrest Park and at the beach. I feel like a field mouse staring up at the jaws of a ravenous bobcat, my feet rooted to the carpet, too frightened to even scream.

Tammy shouts, "Mommy!" again and shrieks so loud I'm sure someone's about to murder my child in her bed.

Hands still shaking from the bizarre dread in the air, I snarl and force myself toward the sound of my daughter's voice. The hallway's become thick with an inexplicable morass of dread. Every inch of motion is a war fought with a heavy, gelatinous resistance that's trying like hell to keep me away from my daughter. Desperation, the need to protect her, rears up within me, a light chasing away the gloom that threatens to ice over my heart. Refusing to acknowledge my terror, I advance toward her door while averting my eyes from the inky cloud still hanging in the living room, unsure why I'm so afraid of looking directly down the hall. My subconscious *knows* death will come for me if I meet its gaze. Nothing matters but getting to Tammy.

I grab the doorjamb and drag myself forward as if out of a tar pit. Tammy's bed stands against the corner of the room; she's curled up against the wall, still screaming as loud as her little lungs will let her. The instant I'm past her door, the bizarre fear evaporates, as well as the force holding me back. Sudden freedom almost causes me to pratfall, but I catch my balance and run to her. As soon as I reach the bed, she leaps into my arms and bawls.

On edge, I spin, cradling her to my chest. Her window's closed, curtains drawn. Closet door is somewhat ajar. Lights are off and nothing appears out of place. My heart still racing, I sit on the edge of her bed, rocking her like a baby while she cries. Her body trembles, which almost makes me wish whatever scared her this badly isn't a nightmare so I can kill it for doing this to her.

"It's all right, Tam Tam. Mommy's here. Bad dream's over."

For several minutes, I keep rocking her, rubbing

her back, and whispering soothing things in her ear. Eventually, her tears peter out to a soft sniveling.

Her face still buried in my shoulder, she mutters, "There's a monster in the closet."

I lift my head to peer at the closet—and the breath stalls in my throat. While the closet *is* empty, the door is now wide open, as is her window. That's not even possible. If some creep had been hiding in her closet, there's no way in hell he could've walked straight past me, opened the window, and climbed out without me seeing him.

Holy shit, my brain is fried. I can't believe what I'm seeing, but I also can't believe her window would've been open. We *always* have the AC on in the summer. With Tammy clinging to me, I approach the window and close it hard before flipping the lock.

"Everything okay?" asks Danny from the doorway.

I yelp and whirl around.

Tammy shrieks.

"Whoa!" Danny jumps. "Sam? What's up?"

"You startled me." I take a couple deep breaths while bouncing Tammy on my hip to calm her down again. "A nightmare."

Only I'm not sure if it's mine or Tammy's.

Chapter Sixteen
Private Eye

I experiment with the metaphysical paradox of being too wound up and freaked out to sleep while simultaneously too exhausted to function. Anthony slept through the whole thing, and even Danny only seemed to notice Tammy screaming. According to him, I walked out of our room and went into hers right away, not the almost five-minute mental battle it felt like to cross ten feet of hallway.

Before Tammy can even ask, I take her to bed with us. Between clinging to her like a frightened child with a doll, and Danny's arm around both of us, somehow, sleep manages to sneak up on me. My eyes peel open a few minutes before my alarm clock goes off. Danny's already in the shower. I sit up, yawn, and nudge Tammy. She's groggy, so I carry her to her room and change her into a cute white sundress with a unicorn embroidery and sandals. Letting her nap a bit more in her bed, I cross the hall to Anthony's room and get him dressed. Ugh. He still hasn't made it through the night without a wet diaper yet, but he's only a few months into being two. Today's an overalls and red shirt day. I'll have to make sure I get some of pictures of him in this outfit to show his future wife. If teenage-Anthony ever finds them, he'll surely delete them.

Danny breezes into the kitchen a few minutes after I have the kids situated with their cereal. "Good morning, sunshine," he says.

Grr. I hate being called that, but I'm far too weary to make an issue of it. "Morning, handsome."

He gives me a quick kiss and fires a mournful look at the inactive coffee machine. Oops my bad. "Got an early meeting with a client today... I'll grab something on the way."

"All right." Screw it. My mental capacity right now is about the same as a five-year-old's; might as well eat like one. I dump more cereal in a bowl for myself and sit down with the kids.

Danny does a circle around the table doing the hug/kiss/goodbye thing with everyone before fast-walking to the door. The scent of his after-shave lingers in my senses; eyes closed, I savor his presence and daydream about that tropical vacation we keep talking about. A whole week together without the interruptions of real life or work. Some day.

Outside, Mary Lou's startled squawk knocks me

back to the here and now. Danny mutters apologies; from the sound of it, he rushed out the door and crashed into her. In seconds, they're both laughing. The *thump* of a car door follows, then the house door closes, and Mary Lou walks into the kitchen, her kids in tow. Tammy waves at her with a giant grin. Anthony blows a milk bubble out his nose.

"The man's in a hurry," says Mary Lou.

"Yeah. Important meeting. You'd think he'd schedule stuff a little later in the day if it's that big a deal."

"Right. Are you okay? You look a little pale."

"Fine. Didn't sleep well." I rub my face. "Watch 'em for a sec, I need to hit the shower."

She nods.

By the time I'm showered and dressed for work, my sister's got the kids in the living room with daytime cartoons on. Usually, I drop Tammy and Anthony off at her place on the way to the office. Her showing up here means she's either intending to spend the day, or she wanted to talk to me. Given the way she's looking at me, I'm guessing the latter.

Mary Lou trails after me into the kitchen when I go to rinse out the bowls... and I find she already did. "Sam?"

"You didn't have to wash my dishes." I smile and turn. "Something's bothering you. Is it that prowler?"

"Prowler?" She tilts her head. "What prowler?"

"The one you saw the other night? Ricky went out to look around and didn't find anything."

She blinks at me, utterly confused. Umm. I did not imagine her calling me in a panic. It's not like her to make stuff up and lie about it. Oh, maybe she's stressed and like sleepwalking or something… doesn't remember calling me.

What the hell is going on?

"I followed Ricky last night. He called me to say he was going out with 'the guys' again. So, I packed the kids in the car and drove to his office."

Wow. That's *way* out of her comfort zone. She doesn't have that kind of nerve before at least two glasses of wine. "Really?"

She leans on the counter, speaking low so the kids don't hear. "Yeah. I was a total mess. I had to know… He didn't go out with the guys, Sam."

My heart sinks. Oh, no… not Ricky!

Mary Lou lifts her head, her eyes reddening in preparation for tears. "He went to this little clinic. A cancer treatment place."

Whoa. Relief that my read of Ricky wasn't wrong crashes headfirst into worry. "Is he…"

Mary Lou shakes her head. "No. When I saw where he was going, I ran in behind him. That mark I thought was a hickey? Well, he thought he had throat cancer or melanoma or something so he went there to get it checked out and didn't want to tell me. He'd been terrified of how I'd react."

I hug her. "You wouldn't have handled it well, but he should've told you."

"How well *can* anyone take that?" My sister shudders, fighting tears. Mary Lou isn't used to being on the receiving end of comfort. She's always the one giving it to others. I don't think she knows how to handle anyone trying to help her or worrying about her feelings. "It's benign, but he's going to have it removed."

Whew. "That's great news."

"Ricky thinks I'm brittle."

I can't help but snicker. "Well… you kind of are. But only superficially. You look like you fall to pieces, but you're strong inside. You had to grow up faster than any of us. I don't know where I'd be without you."

She wipes her cheek. "You know, Mom kinda apologized a couple months ago. I guess she always thought I loved looking after everyone."

"You didn't?" I raise both eyebrows, teasing.

Mary Lou chuckles. "I loved you guys, but seriously, what nine-year-old would rather cook, clean, and take care of her younger siblings instead of *being* a child."

"Yeah. Mom and Dad were more like roommates." Dad spent a good portion of my teen years too high to function after he got released from his position as a minor league pitcher for Rancho Cucamonga. Being unemployed, he had all day to explore parallel dimensions. Mom was always occupied with something: painting, crystals, tarot, reading tealeaves, or just wandering aimlessly among the redwoods. They left the lot of us to our own devices. If not for Mary Lou making sure we got fed, dressed, and off to school every day, we'd have probably wound up like some family on a reality TV show that makes eerie faces at people from deep in the woods. "You did everything."

She folds her arms. "They'd have sooner climbed over trash than cleared out the living room. Clay adored the chaos. He's so much like them now."

Our brother Clayton... he's two years older than me and as much a hippie as our parents were at that age. He *still* has an aversion to pants, and he's shared our father's fondness for weed ever since he snuck his first joint.

"Remember when you found Clay stoned out behind the house? What was he eleven?" I shake my head. "You tried to get him in trouble, but Dad was proud of him for inhaling without choking."

"Unbelievable. I'm *so* glad you never got into that crap. At least Mom mellowed out a bit. She's still with that hotel or whatever." Mary Lou helps herself to a glass of water.

Mom got a job as a docent at some old supposedly haunted hotel. It suits her new-agey personality. She gets paid to wander around and tell ghost stories mixed with history. As far as I know, Dad's co-owner of an 'organic' health food store still. No idea how he got the money for that. As much as he hates the government, I wouldn't put it past him to try and get an entrepreneurial grant. "Dad still doing that Magic Grains thing?"

She nods, drinking.

"Any word from Dusk?" My middle brother. He

didn't go as full-hippie as Clay, but growing up in a household with no structure, no bedtime, and like fourteen years of a shared bed left him permanently averse to order and authority. Last I heard, he somehow managed to get an art scholarship and he's been biking around Europe.

"Not since that email last year with the photos. I think he's still mad at me for trying to talk him out of it and getting a 'real' job. And of course, you committed the ultimate sin."

I laugh. Yeah. Ol' evil me... working for 'The Man.' Clay's the most upset. Last time we were in the same room, he told me I no longer existed to him unless I stopped 'helping the oppressors.' Oy. The boy's smoked himself handicapped.

"River called me last week," says Mary Lou. "He wound up in the hospital."

"What?" I gasp. "You didn't tell me?" River's our oldest brother, one year behind Mary Lou and five older than me. He's always had a problem with self-control, and was in and out of juvenile detention since he was thirteen. At eighteen, he did two years in county for stealing a car to joyride, but he's kept his ass out of jail since. He's been doing rather well for himself as a heavy equipment operator for a construction company. I'm almost jealous really. If I told Danny that my brother made almost twice what he makes and he barely finished high school, I think my husband would have a meltdown. Hooray for unions, right?

"It wasn't that big a deal. He got his foot caught

on his machine and sprained his ankle. Foreman made him go to the hospital for insurance reasons."

"Oh." I sigh silently out my nose while picking a fingernail at the countertop. It's shitty that of my entire family, only Mary Lou really bothers with me. I was always the rule follower as a kid. Not that we had many rules, but I tried to act like the other kids I saw in school who had normal families. "So, Ricky's okay?"

Mary Lou lowers the glass with a gasp of breath. "Yeah. It's benign. We only argued a little. He said he would've told me if it turned out to be cancer, but he didn't want to scare me unnecessarily." Her somber expression curls into a mischievous grin. "I kinda felt like a 'real private eye' there for a while when I was tailing him." She starts to laugh, but it melts into crying.

"Hey…" I hug her again. "It's okay."

"I feel like shit for not trusting him, but I'm pissed off he didn't tell me the truth." She scowls, hands balled into fists. "I don't need to be coddled."

"Men… they think we're all delicate little flowers." I wink. "He did it to protect you, even if it wasn't necessary. I'd forgive him this time, but also tell him he's gotta trust you with the painful stuff too. That's what the whole marriage thing is about."

"Anthony, no!" shouts Ellie Mae from the living room. "Mom! Anthony's touching the mote troller!"

"Shit," I mutter, noticing the time. "I'm late now."

"Mommy?" asks Tammy from right behind me.

"What does shit mean?"

I practically jump out of my skin. Little ninja snuck up on me. Argh! "It's an adult word, okay, Tammy?"

She tilts her head, narrowing her eyes in suspicion.

"It's okay, I got it." Mary Lou hurries to the living room. "What are you doing, Anthony?"

He babbles on about not liking the voice of one of the characters so he wanted to change the picture. This gets Billy Joe and Ruby Grace both yelling that they want to keep watching what's on. I scoop Tammy up and carry her to the sofa.

"I need to go to work now, sweetie."

She hugs me. "Bye, Mommy. Hope you catch the bad guys."

Aww. I ruffle her hair, hover by Mary Lou long enough to kiss Anthony goodbye, and rush out the door.

Chapter Seventeen
The Red Pill

I swing by Starbucks on my way to the office since another ten minutes won't matter. While in line for coffee, I call Nico and tell him I had some family issues to deal with. He's understanding, but his tone suggests a warning not to let it become a habit. Would he give the same attitude to a *guy* calling in late? Of course, being a woman, I'm ten times as likely to let children and home negatively impact work. How dare I reproduce or try to have a life.

Grr.

Relax, Sam.

Nico only sounds mildly annoyed, and it's not like I'm missing a meeting or anything important. Despite the shooter and his friends being in custody, my head's on a swivel as I head outside with my coffee. No one comes after me, and twenty minutes later, I'm safe at my cube.

Chad crosses the aisle, and we chat for a few minutes about my morning. When I tell him about Tammy overhearing me curse, he goes off on this rambling story about his sister's three-year-old who'd evidently spent too much time around Daddy while he sat in traffic. Right in the middle of a supermarket, the precious little girl screamed, "Move you slow piece of shit!" at an old person who got in front of them with a cart.

I'd implode if Tammy ever did that. Lucky for me, she's not a shouter. She tends to get quiet and clingy out in public. Geez, I hope she's not going to turn out to be painfully shy. Another two months, and she'll start preschool. Talking to Chad about how much I'm dreading that first day eats another fifteen minutes.

Eventually, I log into my computer and stare at the list of guys named Haresh Kondapalli. You wouldn't think a name like that would be common, but there are over a hundred in the state. A spark of inspiration hits me, and I add the address from the Newvox account to the search. That narrows it down to one, and I eventually get a social security number. Looks like the guy naturalized in '82. The file photo looks like he's in his mid-to-late twenties. The most current record I can find shows him having moved to Seattle right around the time the house foreclosed. After a few minutes, I find a record of his rental application up there. He started renting an apartment in Washington State five months *before* the bank took over the house here. Weird. Not the best way to pull off an interstate move.

Hmm. I call Corey, the higher-tier rep at Newvox, back; surprisingly, I get through to him.

"Quick question. Can you tell where the physical device is located?" As in, the VOIP device Haresh is using to make calls over the internet.

"Yeah, we can do that by its IP address. One moment." The click of computer keys fills the silence. "Looks like the device is connected to an ISP in the Seattle area."

"Great. Thanks. The warrant for the phone records should be coming back any day now."

"Not a problem, Agent Moon. Whenever you've got it, just fax it in and I'll help you out."

"Will do."

So... Mr. Kondapalli, and his VOIP device, are really in Washington. Well, as Chad would say, that's a wild goose. Maybe I can find something in the paperwork. I pull the HUD application Rosa Melendez filed—this is *so* much easier now that everything is scanned into the computer as images. This job must've totally sucked ten years ago when they had to work with paper all the time. We've still got the original paper of course... somewhere downstairs.

I audit the hell out of it, but don't notice any irregularities. With no better ideas, I pull up Shante Reed's application, hoping to find something there.

After poring over her paperwork for the next twenty minutes, my frustration level is about to send me running for an Advil. Argh. I hate *knowing* there's something off but not being able to pinpoint it. Too many things feel wrong about this entire situation and—

The blur of digitized handwriting sharpens. Wait a minute... Is this Rosa's application or Shante's? I scroll back to the first page and find Shante's name—but the handwriting looks the same. Scooting forward in my seat like an excited moviegoer, I minimize that window and pull up Rosa's documents again. In a few seconds, I've got them side-by-side on my double-monitor display.

I'm sure the same person filled out both of these forms.

"Gotcha!" I say, a little too loud for the office. "Hey, Helling."

Chad rolls back in his chair, sliding into view across the aisle. He must have forty identical sets of baggy white dress shirts and black pants. Today's tie is blue and might be shaped like a Dalek. "Yo?"

"Since when do you say 'yo?'"

He grins. "Since now I guess. What's up?"

"Look at this and tell me what you see?" I point at my screen.

Chad gets up and walks over, trailing the smell of coffee and cinnamon.

"Those things will kill you," I say since I can.

He quirks an eyebrow at me. "What, the cinnamon rolls?"

"They're bigger than my son's head, like 900 calories."

"Calories are only bad if you sit in a chair all day." He leans one hand on my desk, making it creak, and stares at the screen. His head sways back and forth between the monitors for a moment. "Nothing looks wrong."

"You're right. Not *wrong*, but is there something about them that's unusual?"

I resist the urge to hum *Jeopardy* music while he studies the forms.

"Oh… hang on. Looks like the same writing, but two different applicants. Were these apps filed by an attorney? Maybe they hired the same advocate?"

"If an attorney filed this paperwork on their behalf, she or he didn't sign as a preparer. That's a red flag."

He nods.

I pull up Kondapalli's paperwork from five years ago. The handwriting's the same there, too. "Check *that* out."

Chad stands straight and whistles. "Nice. Finally got that fish you've been angling for to bite."

"Something's definitely not right here."

I randomly select forty HUD-managed properties in our area and bring up their paperwork one after the next on my right monitor while leaving Rosa's up on the left side for comparison.

"What are you doing?" asks Chad.

"Where there's smoke, there's fire. If we tripped

over three of these by chance, that means there's gotta be dozens. I think I just found the rabbit hole."

He walks back to his desk for a few seconds and returns. I peer up at him quizzically as he offers me two closed fists. Chad fights not to smile as he opens his hands, palm up, displaying a blue jellybean in his left hand and a red jellybean in his right, Matrix style.

I grab the red one and toss it in my mouth. "Oh, I'm definitely going to see how deep this rabbit hole goes."

Chapter Eighteen
Inspections

A few hours later, I've got sixteen sets of paperwork stacked up on my desk, all filled out by the same person's hand. The tenants don't share any similarities though: men, women, young, old, and multiple ethnicities. About all they have in common is being in financial crisis. Time to follow up on a hunch. I give Nico a brief on what I've found so far, and he's on board with us conducting a few quick inspections.

Our first two visits find locked doors and no answer to knocking or bell-ringing. It's not terribly surprising given it being a little past two. At the third house, a shaggy-haired guy in a Hawaiian shirt shoots us a confrontational stare from a lawn chair. The paperwork says this guy's a combat-wounded vet with a full ride from HUD since he can't work due to his injuries. To look at him, I'd never think he'd been in the military. Long, curly brown-gray hair blends into a matching beard, he's got a not-quite-aware-of-reality look in his eyes, and a belly by Budweiser.

"Whoa. Guess Nick Nolte's fallen off the wagon hard," says Chad.

I chuckle and hop out of the car.

The man's surliness increases as I approach.

"Mr. Mark Beckwith?" I ask.

"I ain't interested in whatever your sellin'. 'Specially if yer one o' them religious types."

"No, Mr. Beckwith." I hold up my ID. "I'm Agent Moon from the Department of Housing and Urban Development. This is my partner, Agent Helling."

He scowls. "You fuckers did enough damage already. Leave me alone."

Both my eyebrows go up. "I'm sorry. What did we do?"

Mr. Beckwith waves his beer around. "Damn government. Ya ripped my ass up already, took mah best years. Can't get in the frickin' door at the VA, and now ya all hasslin' me 'bout the damn house it took an act of Congress to get. Hell, you bastards would have let me rot in that damn refrigerator box forever."

"I'm sorry you had to go through that. If it was up to me, we'd take much better care of our veterans. We're not here to give you a hard time, Mr. Beckwith. It's just a routine property inspection, which your housing agreement mentions. I wouldn't even be here if it wasn't policy. I'm sure everything's just fine, but I'm required to check."

He scowls. "Well, you g'won and look then. My ass is stayin' right here. I'm done humpin' around 'cause the government says so."

"Gulf War?" asks Chad.

Mr. Beckwith nods. "Yeah."

While he reminisces about his time as a ground crewman for an A-10 squadron with Chad, I enter the residence to look around. Normally, these inspections are to check for compliance with the housing agreement. The usual stuff: not using the place for criminal activity, not subletting it, maintaining it in decent shape, and so on. While I doubt this guy's a risk for anything except possible maintenance issues since his mobility's pretty well impaired, I'm here chasing other things.

My first stop is the fridge, but he doesn't have a 'Marty card' on display. It's a little overreaching, but I pull open a few drawers to peek inside without disturbing the contents. Still no luck. A brief walkthrough of the rooms finds nothing out of place. The guy's got so many empty beer cans in his living room that it looks like one of those plastic ball pits kids play in. Wow. It would be a whole afternoon project to unearth the place. Poor guy.

Poor me, too. No luck.

Chad and Mr. Beckwith are in an animated conversation when I return outside. Unfortunately, the tone of it is so aggressively racist against

Middle Eastern people, Chad's responses are all noncommittal noises and grunts. While I can't agree with this guy, I understand how his life of constant, inescapable pain left him bitter beyond reason. Alas, we're not here to pry open closed-mind-edness.

"Mr. Beckwith?" I ask, leaping into a momentary break in his diatribe.

"Huh? Oh, you're back. Find nothin', right?"

I force a polite smile. "Again, I'm sorry for the bother. One question: Have you been approached by a maintenance man named Marty?"

"Nope." Beckwith shakes his head, getting loud. "Ain't no one approach me who got any sense left. Least of all my bitch of an ex-wife and that ungrateful boy." He erupts in another tirade about how he went and 'got his ass blown off' by Muslims to protect this country, and now everyone thinks he's a baby killer. "That boy o' mine ought'a get his ass in a uniform. All you people don't 'preciate that freedom you got on account o' men like me what bled for it. Not so much you, little miss, but this friend o' yours here. You serve?"

Oh, this guy's a graduate of charm school.

"I was still in school when Desert Storm happened, but I gave six years to the Army," says Chad. "Military Police. Didn't see combat though."

"Well, that ain't hardly your fault." Mr. Beckwith mumbles incoherently to himself.

Eager to evade another rant, I thank him for his time and fast-walk back to the car.

"Wow," says Chad, after getting in.

"Yeah. Wow is right." I tap my fingers on the wheel. "I think he's hiding something. You saw how he went off on his ex-wife when I asked about Marty. He wanted to change the subject."

Chad shrugs. "Maybe. Didn't want to press?"

"Not really. I don't think he's going to give up anything useful, not to mention I needed to get away from that rant before I said something unprofessional."

"Can't blame the guy. Radicals messed him up for life."

I pull a U-turn onto the road, and drive back the way we came in. "All modern Germans are to blame for World War II."

"That's not the same thing."

"Isn't it? A small group doesn't make up the mindset of an entire culture."

He scratches at his eyebrow. "I didn't say it's right. I'm saying it makes sense he has that opinion. Bet you ask any World War II vet and they'd feel the same way about Germans."

Shaking my head, I sigh. "That doesn't make it right."

Chad shrugs. "Where to now?"

I pat the stack of manila folders between us. "Pick one."

Chapter Nineteen
Accessories

Our next contestant is Miss Naida Herrera, age twenty-two, who's living in a HUD-managed property in the northwestern part of Anaheim.

Her home is in a dense suburban zone, where the houses are on the large side. The outside is beige, and it's got an attached garage—grr, jealous—at a right angle to the building. Three windows flank the front door, two on the left, and a little Toyota SUV, probably ten years old, sits in a massive driveway that could hold three city buses parked abreast.

Damn, that's a hell of a driveway, but I guess a concrete slab isn't expensive to build. Then again, the place next door to the left also has a damn helipad for a driveway too, so maybe it's the developer.

I pull up and park behind the Toyota. A young

woman with medium-brown skin and thick, black hair peers at us from the leftmost window, tilting her head in confusion, watching us walk up to the door. Since she saw us, I don't bother with the bell, and wait.

The inner door opens a moment later, revealing a young woman in a clingy white t-shirt and denim skirt on the other side of a white screen door. Seeing her barefoot along with the wash of cold air conditioning falling over me makes me shiver. A coo emanates from a tiny infant in her arms. The woman looks nervous, and a couple years younger than her file indicates—or this is her teenaged sister.

"Miss Naida Herrera?"

"Yes," says the woman.

After I introduce us with a flash of a badge, her nervousness blooms into fear. It's not so uncommon for people to react that way when the feds show up, so I try to speak in as calming a tone as possible, and give her the same spiel about routine inspections and I'm sure nothing's out of place.

She nods and backs up, letting us in. I can't resist the baby and spend a few minutes commenting on how cute she is. The infant's too young to tell sex by looking, but the pink blanket's a giveaway. This time, Chad does the walking around while I stay with Naida. Mostly, we talk mom stuff. When she hears I have two of my own, the ice breaks a little. I lapse into sharing some of the funnier moments that happened when they were teeny... like how after I gave a seven-month-old Anthony a bath in a little inflatable tub, I held him up to make silly faces at him, and he peed straight in my face.

Chad walks over to us with an 'everything looks good' expression, but he's also holding a 'Marty card' between two fingers, which he points at me like a gun. "Place is spotless. Looks like there's a man living here as well."

Naida nods. "My husband."

"Yeah, that's on the file." I take the card and show it to her. "Naida, what do you know about this guy?"

"He's who we call if we need something fixed." She shrinks in on herself, breaking eye contact.

Maybe it's not necessarily feds this woman's afraid of. She's small and thin, could probably pass for being a teenager. I feel like Queen Maleficent being forceful with her, but I'm so close to finding a break I have to lean on her a little. Still, I don't have to go straight to threatening her with losing her house.

"Naida, I need you to help me out here. Right now, you're not in any legal trouble. If you're not completely honest with me, that can change."

Her eyes go wide. She bites her lower lip and her toes curl up.

I pull her packet out of the folder. "This is the application you filed for your HUD assistance."

"Okay." She makes a face at it. Either she's illiterate or she's never seen it before.

"This…" I take out Rosa's. "Is someone else's application. The handwriting on both of these forms is identical. That means the same person filled them out. No one signed it as a paid preparer, so either you've filled out a few dozen HUD applications under different names, or you know the person who did."

Naida shakes her head. "I followed all the rules. We're not doing anything against the law here."

Tiny Luisa gets cranky, but calms down when her mother starts bouncing her.

"I'm willing to consider you unaware of what's going on, but if you don't help us, you may be committing conspiracy to defraud the government."

Trembling, Naida looks down and half-whispers, "We followed all the rules. We're only trying to survive and make an honest living. I'm… I don't know why. Can you come back when my husband is home?"

Luisa erupts in a wailing fit. Who says kids can't sense their mother's emotional state. I don't have it in me to badger a young mother cradling her infant. If I can find another tenant who caves in, and I confront Naida with that, I know she'll crumble. I need her on our side, not feeling like she's under attack by the government.

"All right," I say. "What hours is he usually here?"

"After seven. He's working with the telephone company. Up on poles."

Hmm. That job usually pays fairly well, and it's

union. I leaf over their paperwork. It looks like they're getting about 33% assistance, which lines up with the family income level. Nothing is glaring at me here other than her obvious fear when I mentioned Marty.

"We'll be back later. If this Marty threatened you, we can help."

"Oh," says Chad. "We'd appreciate it if you didn't call him and mention we're looking for him. That's a quick way to go from innocent victim to conspiracy charges."

Naida swallows. Hell, it might have even been a gulp.

I make a show of giving Chad a 'that wasn't nice' stare. "Just relax, okay? We're not looking to make your life difficult. My job is to help people in your situation."

She offers a hesitant nod.

Something organized is going on here. In a few days, if I'm still spinning my wheels, I might have to rattle a saber at her. Maybe starting to arrest her would oil her jaw, but the screaming baby's keeping me from going that far right now.

Naida stares mournfully at us from behind the screen door as we walk back to the car and hop in. She looks so much like a teen being abused by a family member, desperate to tell but terrified at the consequences, I'm tempted to hop out and try again. Before I can, she nudges the inner door closed.

"She's being too careful. Someone threatened her."

Chad nods. "Yeah. She's terrified of something. Could be the gang, could be feds. She a citizen?"

"Uhh…" I shuffle papers, hunting for it. "Yeah. Grew up in Oildale."

"Oof," says Chad.

"What?" I ask.

"Not a lot of money out there. Place is a… mess. She's probably suspicious of everyone with a badge."

I drop the car in reverse, sigh, and back onto the street. "Who's next?"

Chapter Twenty
Checkmate

Chad opens the next manila folder, but flips it closed. "How 'bout lunch first?"

"Sure. Can we skip the side of bullets this time?"

He laughs. "Good plan."

We wind up grabbing Chinese takeout. No one interrupts our break with unexpected gunfire, and afterward, we strike out at three more properties where no one's home. Since it feels like we're doing the wild goose chase bit two days in a row, I head back to the office. I could pull every HUD application processed in this area over the past three years, but that would take weeks. My best bet is to wait for that warrant and get the list of phone numbers calling in to Marty's forwarding line, then compare those to our system.

At 4:03 p.m., I'm back at my desk after a quick

meeting with Nico to ask him to expedite that warrant request. He's intrigued by Naida's reaction to my interview, not to mention the matching handwriting on fourteen sets of paperwork. Perhaps adding that tidbit will help the warrant along.

Well computer, I think, staring at my sign-on screen, *do you have any ideas?*

Out of boredom, I decide to keep auditing. Let's see what's going on with Mark Beckwith and Naida Herrera's finances. I'm not expecting to find much in the way of undeclared income, but who knows? Maybe neither one of them are as clean as they look. A quick skim of Herrera's bank history finds nothing alarming like anomalous large cash deposits. There are routine direct deposits from her husband's job, which lines up with the paperwork, as well as mortgage and car payments that stand out as the larger transactions.

Damn.

I pull up Beckwith's account, and he doesn't have any mysterious large sums of money moving around. Just a monthly mortgage—wait a minute… he's got a free ride. His military disability entitled him to a full subsidy of the housing cost, but every month he's got a $300 payment noted as 'house.' I pull up the scanned image of a returned check, and notice he's made it out to MBM Inc. Every month, the same check to the same place.

That's not right.

After going back to Herrera's account, I click on the largest outgoing payment last month, and it turns out to be a check to MBM Inc. I shuffle through her paperwork and find her financials. The property's mortgage payment is $1,856 a month, of which HUD is covering thirty-three percent or $612.48 They should be making payments of $1,243.52, but her checks to MBM are $1,400 on the nose.

A light clicks on in my head. This isn't about drugs. That gang has nothing at all to do with it. 'Marty' is scamming people and using HUD to do it! My theory is confirmed after I check both mortgage histories with the financing banks, and see that they are receiving payments that match the amount on my documentation here. The extra is disappearing between MBM and the bank.

Being the true professional I am, I let out a squeal of delight.

"None of that in the office," says Chad. "At least go to the restroom."

"Very funny. I have a much different squeak for that. Not quite as high pitched and about three times as long. You should hear me when I'm with Danny."

Michelle, who sits to my right on the other side of a tall cubicle wall, giggles. Anders coughs on whatever he's drinking—probably coffee.

Chad slides back in his char to give me the flat eyebrows. I never get tired of the stunned expressions guys put on when a woman throws crudeness right back in their face. "TMI."

"I got something," I say, ignoring him.

"What?" Chad hops out of his chair and hovers over my shoulder while I point out the bank statements.

Rosa's bank account also matches the pattern. She's writing one check a month to MBM Inc. for $150 more than the amount her mortgage ought to be. I check another tenant from the matching-handwriting group, Jessica North, and she's paying $200 over her official mortgage. The next three tenants are all paying from $100 to $250 too much.

"Someone's skimming these people." I slap the folders down on the desk. Now I'm pissed off. "Beckwith's fully subsidized due to his military disability status. He shouldn't have a mortgage payment at all, but look. $300 a month to MBM."

Chad drags his chair across the aisle and sits next to me. "What can we find on this MBM outfit?"

My search turns up that MBM Incorporated is registered as a small home contractor. I can't find a website or any reference to it other than a federal tax ID and a bank account. The address listed for the business is the same as the home address on the VOIP account, the home where Kondapalli doesn't live. My gut tells me Angie isn't involved, though it's probably worth at least a follow-up visit to gauge her reaction to what I've discovered.

Chad whistles. "Wow… Sam, I think you just uncovered one of the biggest HUD scams ever."

"Moon?" asks Nico, his voice coming down the aisle toward us.

"Yeah?" I lean back.

Our boss leans around the opening and hands me a lovely blue folder. "Merry Christmas."

The warrant for the numbers! "Awesome. Hey, Nico…"

He's half a step away, but backs up to peer at me. "What?"

"Look at this." I point at the screens, and explain my theory of someone skimming payments. "He's squeezing our tenants for a couple hundred a month."

Nico leans one hand on Chad's chair, one on mine, and squints at the monitors. "Sweet shit… how extensive is this?"

I *thwap* the warrant against my left hand. "I'm not sure yet, but this should help me answer that."

"Good work. Keep me apprised."

"You got it." I salute him with the warrant. "Be right back. I need to fax this to a man named Corey."

I grab the Post-it note with the fax number for Newvox and jog down the aisle to the copy room to feed the warrant to a machine. Within fifteen minutes, I've got an email from Corey with an Excel sheet attached. Over 14,000 lines of phone numbers. Ugh. I'm about to wail in agony before it dawns on me that there are probably many duplicates. Each line represents a call. They're not all unique phone numbers.

Upon filtering it down to a list of unique values, I'm left with 194 numbers. Time for database crap.

Ugh. I haven't hand-typed a database instruction since college. After creating a new table with the 194 numbers, it takes me about twenty minutes to cobble together a crosscheck query. Let's just say there's a ton of copy/pasting and a lot of leafing through my SQL manual to remember the commands. (There's also a copious amount of foul language the first nine times I try to run the query and it gives me an error over a damn apostrophe being out of place.) Finally, I strike gold.

Eighty-two phone numbers from the Newvox export match the phone number of record for HUD tenants. I cut the list in half, and email one section to Chad.

"Chad?"

"Yo?" he yells, not looking around his cube wall.

"Emailed you something. Can you pull and print the app docs for those accounts? That's half of 'em."

"You got it."

Over an hour of mind-numbing clicking later, I've got a pile of printed HUD applications, all of which appear to have been written by the same person. About twenty percent are no longer active, due to death, incarceration, default, or other various circumstance. Still, they're evidence against whoever this Marty turns out to be.

I dig back into some of the financing banks, and discover that they are receiving payments purportedly through an agent holding a power-of-attorney for the tenants—named Haresh Kondapalli. Looks like Chad and I might be flying to Seattle soon.

Okay. That little more info I wanted before leaning on Naida Herrera? I think I found it.

My turn to roll into Chad's cube. "Come on. We're taking a ride."

Chapter Twenty-One
Pressure Point

Excitement makes it difficult to drive like a normal person. I'm so tempted to hit the lights and haul ass, but no sense risking a reprimand. This isn't a serious emergency, merely a case of nerves. It's still too early for her husband to be home, not quite even three yet, but that doesn't matter with my new information.

Grr. Red lights suck.

"Hey, you're coming next week, right?" asks Chad.

"Depends on how on point Danny is."

"Huh? He usually likes MMA."

I smirk at him. "Swing and a miss, Helling."

"Huh?" His confused, gaping mouth widens. "Oh... right. Geez. I still can't get used to you making sex jokes."

"It's not only men with drive." I wink at him as

the light goes green for us. "So, another match?"

"Yeah. I've got one coming up next Thursday night. I mentioned it the other day, but I guess you were zoned."

Well yeah. "Given that I don't remember it, probably. This case has been keeping me up at night."

"I get it. Anyway, I've got my first official bout coming up."

A lane change is necessary to go around a slowpoke. "But I went to one of your fights already."

"It wasn't ranked. This one's official. I was hoping you and Danny would be up to going and help support me."

"It's not the best place to bring small children." I lean into a left turn. "If my sister's willing to watch them, I'll ask Danny if he wants to go."

"Cool. And it's like wrestling. Kids love wrestling. Lee brings his son all the time."

I shake my head while keeping my gaze fixed on the road ahead. "I don't want to expose my kids to violence like that. They're going to grow up to be well-adjusted adults, not thinking all problems can be solved with violence. And by the way, wrestling is staged. MMA, you guys really knock each other around."

"Aww, you can't shield your kids from real life forever." Chad winks. "But maybe they are a little young to watch MMA."

"Ya think?" I hang a right onto Naida's street.

"And I'm gonna do everything I can to shield them as long as possible. Even if it kills me."

"Supermom."

"Damn straight." I grin. Wow. Figuring this case out has put me in a great mood. I might even get home on time today.

Naida looks less than pleased to see us back so soon, but my big smile must've put her off balance, because she doesn't say a word after opening the door for us.

"I have new information." I pat the manila folder under my arm.

"All right." She backs up, letting us in. "Please be quiet. Luisa's down for a nap."

"Sure," I say in a low voice. "Believe me, I know what that's like."

Chad creeps in behind me and eases the door shut. We gather around her kitchen table, where I lay out the documents regarding her account, as well as a printout of one of her checks, and another showing the deposit amount with the mortgage bank.

"Originally, I thought you might've been involved in some narcotics activity and this Marty person was a contact point. However, I now believe you're the victim of fraud."

She bites her lip again, grabbing the front edge of her chair on either side of her knees. "I don't understand."

"You're making your mortgage payments written out to MBM Inc." I point at the check. "The amount you're paying is $156.48 a month too high."

Chad slides the bank printout over to her. "This shows your payment arriving at the finance bank. They're receiving $1,243.52, but you're paying MBM $1,400 even. Someone is stealing from you."

"And doing it to multiple other people who all have housing assistance through HUD," I add. "I don't mean to scare you, Naida, but if you help conceal this person's activities, we may have to consider you complicit in defrauding the government."

"MBM does not appear to be a legitimate company," says Chad. "I'm with Agent Moon on this. I think you're being taken advantage of, and we'd rather not have you on the hook for conspiracy."

Naida bursts into tears, wrapping her arms around herself and shaking. "Please don't deport me. I'm a citizen! I grew up in Oildale. I'm not from Mexico."

"Hey, hey…" I put a hand on her shoulder. "It's all right. Please calm down. I know you're a citizen. We've already verified that. No one's deporting anyone."

"But… but… he said you would lie and say my birth certificate was fake." Naida looks up at me with such a pitiful, terrified face that she's tripping my mom instincts. I'd have only been nine when she was born, but she's *so* small.

"That's not going to happen, Naida. Please… tell us what happened." I smile as reassuringly as I can.

"But." She looks down. "He said the government would do that if I got caught."

"Caught?" asks Chad. "Caught doing what?"

She opens her mouth, but closes it without a word, trembling harder. I take her hand and we stare into each other's eyes for a moment. Evidently, I'm reassuring enough. She breathes in and out a few times while nodding. "All right. My husband and I... we got this house through a realtor. A man from Fernando's work told him about this guy who can get super low mortgage payments for poor people. The realtor said the government doesn't like the deal he's got, especially for groups they're itching to deport. He told us never to talk about him with any police or government people because they're angry."

"Angry?" asks Chad.

Naida nods. "Yes. Because he has a way to make our mortgages low, the banks don't make as much money, so they are bribing the government to look for any little thing to kick us out and sell the house to rich people."

"Ugh." I rub the bridge of my nose. "You've been lied to, Naida. Do you know what HUD is?"

"That thing like on a military jet, so the pilot can see stuff?"

Chad laughs.

"Well, yeah, technically..." I spend a few minutes explaining how this property has more than half its mortgage paid by the federal government.

"You didn't even realize that, did you?"

"No." She lifts her head hesitantly, peers at me for an instant, and averts her gaze.

"I bet most of these people don't know. If they did, they'd go to HUD directly and avoid being ripped off." Chad grumbles. "Naida, do you know who this guy is? What realtor?"

She nods. "Yes. His name is Martin Brauerman."

"The MB in MBM." Chad grins.

"Where can we find him?" I ask.

Naida scoots back in her chair and stands. "I have his address. He's in LA." She pads across the kitchen to a drawer, rummaging it for a moment before returning to the table with a small address book. "Here." She slides the book to me, open to a page with a number and address. "You're really not going to arrest me?"

"The evidence I have makes me think you're a victim here. Am I going to find anything else that might make me change my mind?"

"No." She's still trembling, but she holds eye contact.

My smile seems to relax her. "Perfect. You should stop making your payments to MBM. This paperwork here"—I pat it twice—"has the correct information and amount. There's a small possibility that after we're done prosecuting this guy, you might recover some of the money that you've been overpaying, but that's largely dependent on what Martin did with it. If it's nowhere the government can seize, it might be a painfully long process and involve you filing a civil suit."

She nods.

"Here's my card. If you have any questions about the paperwork, the process, or anything else about your home, please feel free to call."

"We'll be making contact with all affected homeowners," says Chad. "There's a good possibility you may be called upon to testify at some point during the investigation."

"All right." Naida's almost stopped quivering. She probably won't fully believe we're not going to cart her away in handcuffs until long after we leave.

"Do you have any questions?" I ask, still trying to sound reassuring.

Naida looks over the papers for a minute or two. "Did my husband and I do something illegal? How is this fraud to the government?"

"Technically, your application was in order and you got approved. The fraud here really isn't being committed against the government. *You* are the victim… and everyone else Brauerman has conned. He's taking advantage of people who are barely getting by. That makes it worse to me."

A little warmth shows in her expression at that. "Thank you. We might call after I explain all this to Fernando."

"You're welcome." I stand. "Please don't call Marty and scream at him. If he knows he's busted, he might flee."

Naida narrows her eyes. "I cannot believe he

lied to us with such a friendly smile. He made it sound like he was doing us this great favor. We had no idea how he made the mortgage payment so affordable to us."

"I or my partner will be in contact with you regarding any potential need for you to testify." I stand. "Please call us if you need anything."

Naida smiles, nods, and walks us to the door. "I hope you can make him pay us back."

"That maintenance thing," asks Chad. "Did he actually show up to fix things?"

"Yes. He said he was like a landlord. If the house had a problem, we should call him. Not appliances though."

I frown. "You thought you were renting."

She nods. "We signed some documents at his office, and some weeks later, he showed us this house."

Luisa stirs and makes noise. Naida looks back over her shoulder.

"Your daughter's calling. We need to go anyway." I shake her hand and head back to the car.

"Nice little scam," mutters Chad after getting in. "Figure with around eighty victims, he's pulling in upwards of twelve grand a month."

"Good point. I wonder if he's reporting all that income. Should we send a feeler over to the IRS?"

"Oh, you're evil." Chad laughs.

I put on my most innocent smile. "Not evil. Just thorough."

"You speak of invoking the IRS." He shudders.

"That's evil."

Laughing, I start the car. The rest of the day is going to be fun.

Chapter Twenty-Two
Lorelei Duke

Two days later on Friday, I'm sporting a blonde wig, huge sunglasses, a low-cut top, and a pair of jean shorts that Danny would call 'butt floss' as well as flip-flops. Oh, yeah, I've also got a wire on. This outfit offers no place to hide a weapon, so it's in my purse. Well, not *my* purse, a little hot-pink pleather square from Walmart.

The FBI agent we borrowed to help with the disguise did an amazing job with the makeup and wig. I get mistaken for being in my twenties a lot, but the face staring back at me from the mirror at the office looked more like an eighteen-year-old. We're going for that 'Indiana innocent' thing.

For at least the next few hours, I'm Lorelei Duke, a just-graduated-high-school girl who's moved to California chasing her dream of being an actress. They've set Miss Duke up with a fake job at a nearby go-go bar, though I have no intention of ever setting foot in the place. The manager's cooperative, so if Martin decides to verify anything, he'll be told I'm who I claim to be.

I pull up to a strip mall in downtown LA where Martin Brauerman Realty maintains a small storefront. The hardest part of this operation is going to be not blushing when I get out of the car. The last time I was out in public with this much of my ass exposed, I'd been three years old in my backyard. Well, what passed for a backyard in a trailer park at the edge of a forest. God. Why would anyone wear these things on purpose? It's like having a permanent wedgie.

The agency was even kind enough to procure a disaster of a car: a 1990 Chevy Cavalier that's been to Beirut and back. It smells like I'm sitting in Andre the Giant's sneaker, and the seat is noticeably sticky where it touches my skin. When I get home later, I'm going to soak in a bathtub full of hand sanitizer. The thing runs as smooth as a garbage bag of aluminum cans falling down a staircase. Every head in the parking lot turns toward me, likely expecting a fleet of Hell's Angels.

Fortunately, the car didn't crap out on the short ride, though it doesn't quite want to stop running when I shut off the key. Shit. How am I supposed to kill the engine when the key is already off? It sputters for a few seconds and finally conks out. Well, that's special.

At least it's got cloth seats and I won't leave

skin behind when I stand.

Argh. Seriously. Why do women wear these teeny shorts!? They ride up so snug if I move faster than a walk I think it would count as cheating on Danny. I don't bother locking the door for fear it'll never open again, and walk toward the building. Hell, anyone who steals that car would experience a *loss* of net worth.

Chad was able to verify Martin Brauerman Realty as legitimate. He's a licensed realtor and works officially with non-HUD properties. His little scam with us probably started off as side money, though at this point, he's making more from the scam than his legal commission work.

Predictably, guys stare at me. Yeah, the mostly-open shirt revealing my cleavage is real subtle, but then again, I agreed to do that on purpose. The higher brain functions of most men switch off when a woman shows this much skin. With any luck, if Marty's checking me out, he's not going to be as careful as he might otherwise be. I'm a little pale for this outfit, but that works with the 'just moved here' angle. About all I'm missing is pink bubble gum that I keep snapping. Don't want to push the cliché *too* far. Hmm. Do people from Indiana have an accent? Crap. Oh well, I'll play it as straight as I can.

The girl behind the desk, who probably *is* as young as I'm trying to look, lifts her gaze from a computer screen to smile at me. Her blonde is as fake as mine, but probably triple the cost and from a bottle. A thinly veiled sense of territorial threat bleeds through her expression. "Hello. Can I help you with something?"

"Hi! I'm looking for Marty? I called earlier about gettin' myself a place to live 'round here. You know, it's not rightly nice of me to stay with my friends so long if I can help it."

Great. I come off sounding like Marilyn Monroe on excessive amounts of valium.

"Oh, sure. Miss Duke?"

"That's me!" I grin. "Sorry if I'm a little early. I'm still getting used to this city. Everything's so big! I think you've got more people in one little block than my whole home town."

The woman barely manages to suppress the urge to roll her eyes and nods toward a waiting area. "Please have a seat and I'll let him know you're here."

"Thank you." I wander over to a row of dingy red chairs, looking around, trying to appear awestruck at everything.

"Mr. Brauerman," says the receptionist to her phone. "Your 11 a.m. is here."

An indecipherable murmur emanates from the speakerphone.

"Okay." She looks up at me. "He'll be out in a moment."

"Thank you!" I chirp.

I sit there staring at the bland décor for a little more than ten minutes before a fortyish guy with salt and pepper hair strolls out from an interior hallway. He's wearing a cheap, shimmery gray suit that screams 'used car salesman.' Hopefully, his front desk girl's territorial hostility is only due to her needing to be the prettiest woman in any given place, and not that anything's going on between her and Marty. Of course, if she's eighteen, it's not illegal, but still awkward.

Trying to ignore that unease, I bounce to my feet. "You must be Mr. Brauerman."

"Please." He grins, offering a hand. "Call me Marty."

The elusive Marty. I want to high five someone; instead, I daintily shake his hand. "I'm Lorelei."

"Is that your stage name?" asks the woman behind the desk.

Ooh. Bitch. "Whatever do you mean?" I feign confusion.

She smirks. "Never mind. I thought you were trying to be an actress."

"Oh." I grin. "I am. Just got here two weeks ago from Indiana."

Martin's plastic smile says he probably expects me to wind up hooked on heroin and working in adult films inside of two months. If only that wasn't likely for a girl in 'Lorelei's' position. City of Angels… or shattered dreams.

"Come on back to my office and I'll see what kind of options we have." Martin nods toward the hallway and strides away with a forward-leaning walk.

After an overly polite wave at the front desk

woman, I follow him past a small kitchenette area and a bathroom to the door at the end. His office is large, perhaps a quarter of the whole space, with a window overlooking a row of dumpsters behind the strip mall. What charming scenery.

"Please, have a seat, Miss Duke." He stares straight at my chest as I lower myself into a fake leather seat. "So, how did you wind up hearing about me?"

"Oh, this girl Renata I work with at Diamond's Lounge mentioned you. I'm not sure if that's her real name." A woman he's scamming works there, and her application went through five months ago, so he'll probably assume I mean her. Strippers are notorious for using false names, even to each other.

He nods. "Excellent."

I fidget in the seat, biting my lower lip. "Renata said you can help me get a home, even though I'm not making much money."

Martin observes me, much the way a wolf sizes up an injured deer. While there's a definite sense that he's aroused, the predatory vibe coming off him isn't sexual. In fact, it's pretty tame. He really does feel like a used car salesman about to foist a lemon off on a clueless blonde. "How long have you been in the area?"

"About two weeks."

He jots something down. "And are you working?"

"Mm hmm!" I try to sound impressed. "I'm dancing at Diamond's right now, but it's only temporary until I land an audition. I got the highest score in my drama class at Filmore High, and I was Maria in the school's production of *West Side Story*. Mr. Benson told me I'm gonna be a star someday." I can picture Chad, outside somewhere listening to my wire, rolling his eyes and laughing.

Martin cringes. He almost seems sorry for me, but his smile returns. "Well, in addition to being a realtor, I run a property management company on the side. I specialize in helping people in your... income bracket obtain housing. Now, since you're likely to wind up a famous actress before too long, I'll probably have to assist you finding a more fitting home someday, but until then, I think I can probably help you."

"That's swell!" I grin. Do people in Indiana still say 'that's swell?' Hope so.

He fishes around a lower drawer in his desk and hands me three stapled bundles of paper, standard realtor dossiers on houses for sale. "Take a look at these. I think they're the ones most likely to fall within your budget. I can't make any promises. The final determination happens with the bank, but I'll damn sure fight hard for you."

"Hmm. They're all so pretty." I read the addresses aloud so we get them on tape, and giggle. "Oh, Mr. Brauerman, I don't know any of these street names. What are the areas like? They're not full of bad people, are they?"

"Oh, no... they're all in nice areas. A pretty little angel like you shouldn't have any problems."

"That's good to know." I hold up the cheapest one and sit with a posture that makes my chest prominent. "I think I better try for this one. I'm not making an awful lot of money right now. But as soon as I get into the movies, I won't have to worry about money."

Martin grins. I can practically see the dollar signs in his eyes. "All right." He hands me a clipboard with some forms. "If you wouldn't mind, please fill those out and I'll get things sent to the bank right away."

The forms look like a rearranged version of the HUD application. Naturally, he's collecting all the information so he can fill out the real documents. I spend a few minutes filling stuff out, regurgitating all the information I rapidly memorized earlier when we cooked up the Lorelei Duke persona. If, as we expect, he's going to feed this back to us, we can fix anything I don't get quite right. Every three or so lines, I ask basic questions about what I'm supposed to put there. It makes the process tedious, and gets him red-faced with frustration, but each time he's about to snap, a boob wiggle distracts him. Okay, maybe this is overdoing it. I don't need to make him think I've got the IQ of a scallop, but if I filled this thing out like a pro, he'd get suspicious.

Once I have all the sheets finished, I hand the clipboard back to him. "I think that's everything. Are you sure this is going to work? I thought getting a place would be a lot more work than filling out some forms."

Martin mutters, "Oh, don't worry. That's what I'm here for," while looking over the information. "Everything seems to be in order here." He lets the papers flutter flat against the clipboard and smiles at me. "This number you put here as your contact. That's a cell phone?"

"Uh huh." I nod. "I can take it with me wherever I go."

His 'holy crap this girl's an airhead' expression almost gets me to laugh. "Umm. Yes, well. That's the whole point of cell phones." The smile returns. "I'll see what I can do with this and give you a call in a couple days once I get an answer from the bank. On your way out, stop by Marissa's desk so she can take photocopies of your driver's license and Social Security card."

"Oh, great. Thank you, Mr. Brauerman!"

Martin stands and walks around the desk. "Please, call me Marty."

I'm expecting a pat on the ass as soon as I stand, but he surprises me by behaving himself. The receptionist narrows her eyes ever so slightly when I flounce across the lobby and approach her. Ice hangs in the air while she takes the fake license and SSN card to copy, practically throwing them at me when she's done.

"Thanks," I chime, overacting innocence.

Marissa narrows her eyes, but keeps a forced smile. "Have a nice day."

Outside, two guys whistle at me, one yells, "dat ass!" and another rides his skateboard straight into a post along the strip mall frontage.

Laughing, I stroll back to the POS car, certain Marty is watching me. The door creaks when I open it, and the engine doesn't want to start, but at least getting in makes me feel less exposed to the world. After much banging and swearing, it finally turns over, and the roar of a dead muffler follows me out of the parking lot.

I can't wait to get back to the office and out of this ridiculous outfit. Hopefully, it won't take Marty too long to submit the paperwork while claiming to be me, or rather Lorelei. It's petty, but I think I'm going to enjoy watching the receptionist flip out when we swarm the place.

Chapter Twenty-Three
Done Deal

The rest of Friday passes in a blur of collecting documents, bank statements, and every scrap of paper trail I can get my hands on into a neat package before forwarding it on to the federal prosecutor.

I'm only a little late getting home, but I've got a giant, satisfied smile. Mary Lou's agreed to keep the kids overnight so Danny and I can go out. We have a wonderful time at a nice sit-down Mexican restaurant, and catch *The Bourne Supremacy* after since it's opening today. When we get home, we make love like we just got married, and wind up falling asleep naked together.

This is payback weekend, and not in a bad way. While Danny keeps an eye on our kids, I drive over to Mary Lou's to pick up her three. I'm watching her brood until Sunday night. She and Ricky are going off to some cabin he's got in Big Bear for some 'couple time.'

For the most part, the weekend is a blast. Juggling a pair of two-year-olds is a challenge in public, but we hit the Universal Studios Hollywood park on Saturday, and The California Science Center on Sunday. It's tiring, but amazing. I think Anthony and Ruby Grace are conspiring to take over the world. Every time I look their way, they're muttering to each other and eyeing the world around them like they're up to no good. Ellie Mae is a lot like her mother. Even at six, she's trying to help me take care of the smaller kids as much as she can.

Sunday night arrives too fast, and I'm almost sorry to see my sister's kids go.

Danny sidles up behind me while I stand in the door watching Mary Lou pack them in their minivan. He kisses the side of my neck and asks, "What's wrong?"

I lean into him. "I expected this weekend to kick the crap out of me, but it was fun. Wrangling five wasn't as bad as I thought."

"Maybe in another life you had a huge family and a part of your soul misses it."

"When did you turn into a mystic? That sounded scarily like something my mother would've said." I wave to Ricky and Mary Lou as they back out of the driveway.

Danny pulls me inside and nudges the door closed. "You're not pondering another one, are you?"

I grab my belly. "Oh, I don't think so. I haven't been at HUD that long and if I go out on maternity leave, well, they might find an excuse to cut me loose."

"Hmm. So, if I knock you up, you might be forced to do something that won't expose you to bullets?" He grinds against my butt.

"Hah! Keep that thing away!" I laugh, playfully trying to twist my rear end out of stabbing range.

Anthony lets off a shrill glass-shattering shriek that fills the hallway. He's never made *that* sound before. Panic fills Danny's eyes. Wordless, we both run toward the sound of screaming child—and find our son stuck in the toilet, almost folded in half.

"Ooh. That water's cold, isn't it, little man?" asks Danny.

I put a hand over my mouth to stop from laughing. That noise he made sounded like he'd cut his foot off. Danny lifts the wailing boy out of the toilet and sets him in the tub for a quick bath.

"Might as well kill two birds," I mutter, and head off to collect Tammy.

When I set her in the bathwater Danny's run, he looks up. "She's probably getting a bit old to share a bath with him."

"She's only four." I put my hands on my hips.

"How old were you when you stopped sharing a bathtub with your siblings?"

I laugh. "You don't want to know."

He stares at me. "Wow, really?"

"Uhh, like nine..." I squint, trying to remember

exactly when my demand for privacy got heeded. Probably as soon as I could run the bathwater myself. "We were kinda backwoods in those days."

"Surprised CPS didn't take you away." Danny washes a squirming Anthony.

I soap up Tammy's hair. "Oh, if they ever came out to check on us, they would have. We looked like a Great Depression family for a while there."

"Sorry," says Danny.

"Oh, it's not that bad. We had plenty of food... just wasn't the cleanest place to live."

He nods. Danny's childhood was painfully normal. His older sister Julianna moved to the east coast. She's a prosecutor somewhere in Maryland, trying to get into the federal circuit. His younger sister Adriana is an absolute doll. I think she absorbed all the 'nice' between the two girls. If a guy mugged her and tripped while running away, she'd run over to help him. She's twenty-five now I think, with the same dark hair and blue eyes as Danny. Started off as a social worker, but she couldn't handle the depression. Cried herself to sleep every night after some of the situations she had to deal with. Poor girl didn't last a year. She's a teacher now up in Glendale, working with K through fifth-grade.

Danny's somewhere between the two extremes. He can have Adrianna's loving kindness at home, but he usually turns into Julianna in the courtroom. Not that she's wicked or anything, but she's got the ability to switch off empathy. Danny sometimes calls her 'the android.' Fortunately, she's more a rule follower than even I am, so if she *is* a sociopath, at least she's a sociopath for the forces of good.

Anthony's fidgety on the way to bed, but Tammy's out in my arms before I can even get halfway to her room. With the kids tucked in, Danny and I have some wine in the living room, smooch a little, and migrate to the bed for some heavy cuddling. I love that so much about him. Sometimes, he just wants to hold me and be close.

Laying there in Danny's arms, I let my mind drift over all the fun memories we made this weekend, even if three of the children involved aren't mine. Still, they're family.

A contented sigh escapes me as I snuggle up to the man of my dreams.

I am a lucky woman.

***

The alarm slaps me awake, still in my clothes except for shoes. Danny stirs and groans, rolling onto his side while clutching his arm. His right hand is as pale as a snowman, and about as dead as one.

"Sorry," I mutter.

"Not your fault." He grits his teeth as pins and needles come on.

The morning is as normal as things can be. A shower, change, and breakfast later, I'm in the momvan driving the kids to Mary Lou's on my way to the office. Another long day of pushing paper back and forth has a welcome break around one in the afternoon when Chad and I head to the hospital to confront the kid who tried to shoot me at Nick's Super Burger. Sure enough, it's him. The little bastard's defiant. Won't even look me in the eye. Alas, I can't ID the other two since I only saw one with a bandana over his face. I only got a glimpse of the other one's hand when he pulled the shooter in the fleeing car. Confirmation of the one is enough though, since the lot of them had blood all throughout the car, and the ballistics from slugs recovered in the car and the suspects matched our Glocks. Between Chad and I, we hit them almost twenty times. The shooter will be stuck in bed for a while due to a shattered hip, and he's missing part of a kidney. Back seat guy lost a finger, and the driver took a handful of superficial wounds. They'll all live.

Speaking of living, Rosa Melendez pulled through. We visited her after the ID session, and she finally admitted the truth about Marty once I told her we'd found him. She'd already figured out he'd done something shady with HUD, but she'd been afraid we'd charge her for not reporting it. It'll take her a couple weeks, but the doctors think she'll get back to normal. The slugs they pulled out of her back matched the .32 revolver used by the baby-faced man who tried to kill me at the burger place. Chad thinks he's going to make some guy in prison very happy.

***

Wednesday at 10:08 a.m., Lorelei's cell phone rings. I clear my throat and try to channel my inner airhead. By the way, Chad said I sounded like Brittany Spears on Ecstasy. The guys in the surveillance van were laughing themselves to tears the whole time listening to me with Brauerman.

"Hello?" I ask, settling on 'timid and ditzy.'

"Miss Duke?" asks Martin Brauerman.

"Oh, hi!" I chirp. "Marty?"

"That's right. I have great news! The bank approved the financing for your place. Come on in and we can discuss everything. If you like what you see, we can sign the papers and get things rolling."

"That's awesome! I can be there in like two hours, is that okay?"

"One moment, let me check my schedule…" He's a hard mouse-tapper. "Two hours is fine. See you at noon."

"Okay." I add a trace of giggle.

The vapid voice gets Chad peering at me around his cube wall.

As soon as the call ends, I wave the cell phone at him. "Fish on the hook. Got an appointment with him at noon. I am *not* wearing those shorts again."

"Aww." He snaps his fingers in an overacted display of disappointment.

After I tell Nico I got the call, he pulls us all into a conference room to run over a briefing. I'm (obviously) going to go in again dressed up as

Lorelei. As soon as Martin commits to the offer and has me sign paperwork, the other agents are going to rush the place. We've got several warrants waiting already to raid every file cabinet and nanometer of hard disk space in his realty company.

Other HUD agents in the Seattle area have already interviewed Kondapalli, who turned out to be another victim. He's in country on a work visa doing programming, and thought he'd been renting the place from Marty not realizing he had a HUD mortgage. When his job ended and he found a new one in Seattle, he told Marty he was moving and took off. Brauerman wound up hacking Haresh's Newvox account and added a second line.

Anders, Rivera, and Montoya will wait outside the place and we'll have one LAPD unit on hand for additional security.

"Sounds pretty straightforward." Nico nods at no one in particular. "This is about as clean and easy as it gets, but don't let your guard down. This guy might have a gun tucked away somewhere."

Murmurs of agreement come from everyone.

"Thanks guys." I stand. "Guess it's time for sexy pants."

They all clap, except for Nico, who pats me on the shoulder. "Really nice bit of investigation there, Moon. Brauerman covered his tracks pretty well."

"Ehh. I got lucky. Looked at two records back to back and happened to notice the handwriting matched. Oh…" I flash a cheesy smile at Montoya. "I found something else."

The room goes pin-drop silent.

"All but a few recent tenants were part of Donnie Vento's caseload," I say.

Everyone cringes like I just shouted 'Voldemort' in Hogwarts. Vento caused so much havoc here, he's become the agent who shall not be named.

"I wonder if he might've been working with Brauerman," I say.

Nico gasps. "That would make so much sense, but I think Vento was just an idiot... but if he is complicit, I think the team will erect a statue in your honor."

Montoya stares at me in wonderment for a long minute before stating in a matter-of-fact tone, "I am going to kiss you full on the lips."

"Sorry, Ernie." I wag my wedding band at him. Oh, shit. I gotta take that off again for the undercover. "I'm taken."

"If he's involved in this, you'll never pay for lunch again as long as you work here," says Montoya.

Rivera and Anders nod.

I laugh. "I can't take that much from you guys. I'll settle for one nice dinner."

"And you shall have it." Anders bows like a knight to a queen.

Heh. What a pack of oddballs.

***

A few minutes before noon, I limp that old Cavalier into the parking lot by Martin's office.

Today's outfit is far more functional than last time: jeans, sneakers, and a loose flannel shirt over a sports bra. The unbuttoned front shows enough skin to keep Marty distracted, but it hangs low enough to hide the holster behind my back and the handcuff case next to it. As long as I don't do jumping jacks in there, they should remain out of sight.

My tight jeans cause some stares on the walk to the door, but the reaction is much tamer than last time. The receptionist gives off three seconds of an 'oh, it's you again' smirk before putting on her work smile.

"Hi again. Can I help you?"

You know, I probably *could* be an actress. I grin at her like I'm thrilled to see her. It's easy to fake since in an 'I know something you don't know' kind of way, I *am* happy. "Marty called me and said I had to come in to sign some stuff. I have like an appointment at noon."

She looks at her computer. "Oh, I see it. I'll let him know you're here."

"Thanks." I take a seat while she sends him an IM or something. At least I assume so since she doesn't call him.

Marty appears in the hallway a minute later and waves me to follow him. "C'mon back."

I grin and scurry after him. It's not too difficult to act excited, only a new house on the cheap isn't

223

the present under my tree. Martin pulls one of the leather chairs out for me before going around his desk to sit.

"I must say I'm pleasantly surprised. Given your income level and... well... if I may be blunt, your background, I'd expected to have to fight a little harder for you."

"Oh." I blink, acting innocent. "Is that bad? What's wrong with my background?"

He waves dismissively. "I've found a certain loophole in the finance industry that allows me to help people out who are in your situation. It's obscure, and not too many know about it. The way it's designed, it's... look, Miss Duke, I won't mince words. It's set up to benefit those of a somewhat darker persuasion."

I fake a sneeze to hide the glare I felt forming. This'll be even more satisfying. Not only is he skimming off people, he's a bigot. One of those people who buys into that conspiracy HUD exists to seed minorities in 'communities too good for them.'

"Bless you," says Martin.

"Sorry." I wipe at my nose. "Oh, I get it. But why would the bank be nicer to me if I was like Hispanic or something?"

He shrugs. "Affirmative action and whatnot."

"Oh." I play dumb, like he thinks I am. "I don't really understand what that is." It's difficult to conjure a vapid smile, but I manage. "I'm glad they said okay. That's affirmative, right?"

His smile falters. For an instant, I get a pitying

stare before his saccharin grin returns. "I am quite glad as well. A promising young actress like yourself deserves a safe place to sleep! The city can be unkind enough to the innocent. I'm glad I can help keep you secure at night."

"Oh, thank you, Marty. You're so sweet." I fidget. "Umm. So, how does this work?"

"Well." He pushes some papers across the desk to me. "Here are the documents. Your monthly rent payment will be $550. I realize that's about two weeks' pay for you, but it's as low as I could get it. Now, one thing I can suggest is for you to get a roommate. But, if you do that, you'll need to be careful."

"Oh, yes. What if they turn out to be a creep or a psycho." I nod.

He chuckles. "Well, that too, but I mean, if anyone from the government ever shows up, you can't tell them you have a roommate. They know about the loophole I use and they look for any technicality to kick people off that plan. Whenever I rent to someone in your position, they like to show up and claim they can inspect the place. It's better to let them do it, but don't admit to the roommate. Tell them it's just a friend visiting. Normally, they get deportation happy, but you won't have that problem. But, they *can* evict you and revoke the whole deal if they think you have any extra income, and having someone else there to help pay your rent counts as income."

"Oh." I flash my best 'someone shot my dog'

expression at him. "Isn't that like against the law to lie to the government?"

He shakes his head, grinning. "No, no, my dear. They're just inspectors. Guys in suits with nothing better to do than hassle people who don't make much money. An extension of the big banks who want wealthy people to get in the door of your house so they can make more money. It's all one big, corrupt machine."

"That's sad."

"Yeah it is, but you're one of the little people, Miss Duke. Don't let the government push you around. They only care about corporations and banks. Now…" He slides another paper over the desk toward me. "The way my special arrangement with the lender operates, you'll be making your rent payments to my property management company, MBM, Inc. You won't need to worry your pretty little head about anything else. Leave the worrying to me."

I let out an airheaded giggle. "Okay. That's so sweet of you!"

"Any questions?" asks Martin, toying with a pen between his fingers.

"Umm. If I'm renting from you, what's a bank involved for?" I ask, laying on the innocence.

He smiles. "It's a requirement in California. Think of it like a credit card. Before I can get the approval to take on a new tenant at your income level, I need to convince a bank to secure the rental in case something unfortunate happens. That way the property's taken care of until a new tenant can take it over."

"Oh. I'll try not to miss any payments."

Martin takes out a packet with some more pictures of the house I picked. Monday, the HUD paperwork came in like Lorelei Duke submitted it herself, and the handwriting matched the others. The property I selected is in a depreciated area, so it's not too expensive for California. The full mortgage is $880 per month and HUD is covering $600 of it. I *should* be paying $280, but Marty needs his $270 cut. Wow, this guy's got no qualms stealing most of an eighteen-year-old aspiring actress' pay for a week. The way he's smiling and acting all warm and protective makes my skin crawl. How many other Lorelei's have been in this chair feeling like they've just gotten the break of their lives?

"Okay, so all I have to do is sign this here and I'm renting this house from your management thingee?"

"That's right." He grins. "It will take a few weeks for me to hammer out the legal stuff in the background before you can move in. Do you have a checking account?"

I nod. "Yeah. My mom got me one when I turned sixteen."

"That was nice of her. Gotta teach financial responsibility to kids these days. To continue, we'll need a check to cover the first month's rent, plus a $175 document processing fee. I'd waive that if I could, but it's going to the government. They never miss a chance to take a bite out of our butts."

"Yeah." I fake a frown. "Stupid government."

Chad and the others are probably laughing their asses off listening to me.

Martin taps his fingertips together, looking concerned. "Is that something you can swing?"

"Umm. $550 plus $175... that's like six hundred... no. Umm. I'm not good at math. Sorry." I grab his pen and scribble random numbers for a moment. "Oh, $750?" It's actually $725, but I want to see what he says.

"You got it." He grins. "See? You're not that bad at math."

I wince. "I didn't bring my checkbook. Like no one ever uses them anymore."

"Oh, that's all right. This is going to take a couple of weeks anyway. You can drop the check off any time, though the sooner you do, the faster things will start. There's going to be a rental approval meeting in a few weeks where you'll need to sign a bunch of paperwork. Again, it's a formality the government requires. It's important that you don't say anything about our arrangement, just sign where they tell you to sign. I'll be right there with you as your realtor."

"Okay." I scoot forward and grab the pen from the desk. "So, I need to sign this and I'll have my own place? Well... rental anyway."

"Right." Martin leans over his desk and points out where I need to sign.

This is all some kind of weird formality. He's already forged my signature with HUD. As far as the bank is concerned, this deal's already on its way to closing. I scribble a giant, girly L with an indecipherable squiggle after it as a signature, and spend the next few minutes initialing here and there where he points. Right when I think I'm done, he points out another eight places for me to sign. Geez. This is giving me flashbacks to when Danny and I bought our current house. I'm basically filling out a mortgage form, but he's got little green Post-it arrows covering certain critical things like the word 'mortgage' and 'housing assistance,' and of course, the true payment amounts.

Wow, I guess no one really ever looks at what they sign. The true amount was right in front of everyone's nose and they didn't catch it. Or maybe the ones who did ran for the hills? Anyway, I eventually finish signing the whole thing and lean back in the chair acting exhausted.

"Wow that was a whole lot of signing."

He chuckles condescendingly and winks. "Well, don't worry your pretty little head about anything. In a month or so, you'll have a nice house to move into."

"Is that it? Are we done?"

"All set… uhh, except for your first deposit. Drop it off with Marissa as soon as you can and I will call you to let you know when the review meeting is."

"Okay." Wow, it's exhausting pretending to be

an airhead. "Time to move in."

Martin stands and offers a handshake over the desk. "Not quite yet. Won't be moving day for about four weeks."

"That's not what I meant, Marty." Samantha Moon's smile emerges from under the Lorelei veneer. I take his hand and shake. The strength of my grip catches him off guard. Martin's eyebrows rise in time with the squeak of the front door opening. A quick tug and spin pulls him over the desk like a landed fish. I swoop around to pin the arm behind the back, and tug the badge out of my pocket.

"What the hell are you doing?" shouts Martin.

Marissa shouts, "Hey, you can't just go back there!" followed a second later by, "Get off me!"

I lean my weight on him and hold the badge where he can see it. "Federal agent. Martin Brauerman, you're under arrest for wire and mail fraud, forgery, and conspiracy to defraud the federal government."

Martin struggles as I try to get the cuffs on him, but goes still when Chad and Bryce Anders stride into the office, their badges obvious on their belts. "Fuck…"

"That's one way to put it," says Chad.

I haul Martin up from the desk and guide him over to Chad before pulling the blonde wig off. "Damn this thing itches."

Marissa, seated in the back of a LAPD car, shakes and sobs. We're just borrowing the car for the moment until we figure out if we're detaining her on a more permanent basis. When I walk out front, she looks up and stares at me in shock. Her jealousy's out the window, and she gives me this pleading face. Okay, my cattiness curls up to take a nap.

Bryce and Montoya load Martin into one of our fed SUVs.

"Chad? You mind overseeing the search for a little while. I want to interview the receptionist. Something tells me she's probably not involved."

"Knock yourself out." Chad gestures at the car.

Crap. I have to remember how the Miranda warning goes.

Chapter Twenty-Four
Every Precious Second

Wednesday night, I can't sleep. Danny's long since passed out beside me. The kids are tucked in and comfy, and here I lay, staring at the ceiling with too much adrenaline to let me close my eyes. I'm excited, happy, and relieved all at once. I got home late, but it was worth it.

Marissa claimed not to know that Martin ran a scam on the side, but she did suspect something weird might be going on given all the "poor people" who showed up at the office. She didn't set off my BS detector, so I cut her loose and warned her to stay in the area in case she's needed at Martin's trial. Unfortunately, she's also unemployed now.

We spent the remainder of the day boxing documents and computer equipment and humping it all back to our field office. The next few weeks are going to be tedious, but rewarding. I think my favorite part will be going out to the properties and telling people they've been ripped off. Citizens don't mind feds so much when we bring *good* news.

Ugh. I need to burn off some of this excess energy or I'm never going to be able to sleep.

Careful not to disturb Danny, I slip out of bed. Usually when I need to clear my head, I go jogging around Hillcrest Park, which is a short distance down the road from our house. A few minutes past eleven at night isn't exactly the greatest time for a run, but this area's pretty free from crime. I'm also a trained federal agent with a gun. I'm no Jackie Chan, but I can hold my own against punks.

I change into my running shorts, a tank top, and sneakers before slipping my shoulder holster on. Might as well wear my badge on a chain around my neck in case a random cop decides to give me the third degree for having a Glock.

After kissing the sleeping Danny, I head out into the hall and creep into Anthony's room with the stealth of a ninja. Well, at least a thirty-one-year-old suburban mom version of a ninja. He's out like a light, mouth open, "catching flies" as my husband would say. I snug his blanket up, give him a kiss on the cheek, and cross over to Tammy's room. She's gotten in the habit of sleeping on her left side in a fetal position. It's adorable, but it makes me wonder if she's having bad dreams. Her lack of squirming or making noise eases that fear, and I give her a kiss on the head.

Keys, check. Cell phone, check.

Okay, guys. Mommy will be back in a few minutes. Just need to tire myself out or I'm going to be awake all night.

The July night is warm and dry, the moon bright in a cloudless indigo sky. Stepping out of air conditioning makes it feel warmer than it probably is, but by the time I'm back, I'll be more than ready for AC. After doing a few stretches to limber up, I head off to the left, following the road up toward the woods—or what passes for woods in Fullerton—at the park.

Our neighborhood is quiet, save for a single barking dog somewhere behind me. Houses go by, some with lights on, most dark. Guess people around here don't burn the midnight oil very much. At the end of Shady Brook Drive, right before the little spur connects to Lemon Street, repetitive high-pitched squeaking echoes from a bedroom window. Everything inside glows blue from a television screen, which paints the shadows of a man and a woman going at it on the wall.

Nice. At least close the curtains.

I cut over the spar and jog past Lions field, running along a thin strip of trees that separates it from the road. Lemon Street will take me to the park entrance, opposite where Virginia Road cuts off to the right. That's a nice curving path around the woods. I keep saying woods, but I really shouldn't call a section of trees like 150 feet wide and 600 feet long "woods." It's not even close to the forest around where I grew up. But still, it's nice scenery.

Or it used to be. I can't help but think about that strange night when I lost my sense of direction in such a small patch of wilderness. I've been jogging around this area for years, and I've spent my fair share of time going into the trees as well. I don't remember them being that thick, nor that dense. The more I think about it, the less sense it makes that I could've gotten disoriented.

Whatever. Had to be stress. I stop trying to think about anything and focus on the mechanics of jogging: breath flowing in my lungs, blood coursing through my veins, the rhythmic thudding of my sneakers on the pavement. All the stress of the investigation is over. I take a huge breath in my nose and let it out my mouth, visualizing worry and anxiety extruding from my body along with it.

An unusual sense of apprehension draws my attention toward the trees again. Though I don't see anyone, it feels like I'm being stared at. Maybe it's that homeless guy that ran away when we had the blowout? It couldn't be that gang, could it? Inexplicable malice radiates from the darkness between the trees, adding urgency to my stride. Without even thinking, I go from jogging to a light run. Maybe I should've stayed inside.

Come on, Sam, don't flake. I've got training and a weapon. Still, the unsettling feeling that something is extremely wrong won't leave me alone. I slow to a stop, breathing hard, and scan the woods. It's oddly dark despite the full moon, but nothing's moving. That strange, paralyzing fear that hit me here last time—and again in my house when Tammy screamed—doesn't happen again, but the memory of it haunts me enough to tighten my airways. It makes no sense at all, but I feel like I'm being stalked.

Oh, hell with this. Time to go home. Maybe I've got a migratory blood clot or something from that bruised rib and it's screwing with my brain, making me hallucinate things. Tomorrow, I'm going to at least talk to a doctor.

I hurry back along the road with the trees on my left. Each time my sneaker pounds pavement, my need to get home builds. Before I know it, I'm near to sprinting with no idea what I'm running away from. At the moment, I don't care if I'm going crazy, I need to get home, back to my family.

A curve in the path ahead comes up fast. Usually, I'd take the left turn about halfway around the bend then loop around the big round field, but screw it. I'm heading straight through the trees back to Lemon Street.

Seconds away from reaching the bend, the world becomes a blur. Stars and road flash by in my vision along with a sense of flying. Not a sense—I *am* flying. A tremendous *crack* rocks my body as I slam into something hard and collapse to the ground, staring up at the tree I just crashed into. I can't tell if the tree broke or if the snap came from my spine.

"Ugh."

Sprawled on my back, I can't summon the will to move at all. I merely breathe hard in silence. Seconds tick by before the pain starts, worse than the bruised rib. A strangled scream leaks past my teeth. Did I get hit by a car from behind? Except I'm in the woods, still far enough not to see the road. Yet...

Yet I must have flown twenty feet or more.

Not flown, I think. Hit...or thrown. Something's out here.

I manage to straighten my left leg. Good. Back's not broken, but even that motion triggers searing agony. A shoe scuffs dirt behind me, lighting off an explosion of panic. I gasp and grunt, trying to get my arm to cooperate and reach across my chest for my weapon. Dammit! Why can't I get up! Involuntary tears roll down my face, whether from fear or pain I can't tell. Oh, damn this hurts. I bet I've got broken ribs on both sides this time.

A deep, bestial snarl rumbles in the dark.

Shit!

Forcing my hand closer to my Glock feels like I'm splitting my back open, but I keep trying. Sweat runs into my eyes and the taste of blood leaks into the back of my throat. Oh, shit. That's a punctured lung. No wonder I can't breathe. Ngh! Come on. I can get help. Just need to fire a couple bullets into the dirt. Someone'll hear it and call the police.

I can't help but scream as I force my arm the last few inches. The instant my fingertips touch the gun, a man's sinister laugh slithers out of the night from about twenty paces. Gasping in pain, I force my grip closed on the handle. Before I can draw the weapon, a man pounces on me with such force we go sliding away from the tree over the dirt.

The pain that blasts my shoulders and back rips a jagged scream from my lungs and leaves me seeing a blur of white spots. A glimmer flashes before my eyes. Time drags to a standstill as a beautiful ruby and gold medallion dangles in front of me. Tranquility lasts a mere second, destroyed when a sharp, penetrating pain spreads over the side of my neck. A feeble squeak leaves my throat, melting into a wet gurgle. I gag, choking, coughing, and spitting out blood.

Slurping fills my right ear along with squishing, and the grinding of teeth on bone. I'm dreaming. I'm having a nightmare. This jog isn't happening. *This* isn't happening. I'm still lying in bed with Danny. No one's cutting my throat open in the middle of Hillcrest Park at midnight. That sort of thing doesn't happen around here. Not to a federal agent.

The empty sky fades away. I'm standing in Mary Lou's house, watching my sister have a panic attack in her hallway. I think she's staring into Ruby Grace's bedroom. The little girl's screaming for her mother, but Mary Lou backs away, an expression of abject terror on her face. She runs off down the hall, leaving the child to scream.

Darkness.

The hallway right outside my bedroom door

fades in. I'm standing at the end of the hall near the living room, watching myself walk out of the bedroom and freeze in fear. Tammy screams for me. I want to get to her, more than anything in the world, but this bizarre visioning won't let me move at all. Not-me growls and advances into the hall, wild-eyed and feral, dragging herself into Tammy's bedroom.

Everything fades, leaving me gazing up at star-flecked indigo once more.

My breaths come shallow, gurgling. I can't feel anything. No pain, only the soft coolness of the ground at my back. A baffling sense of disdain fills me toward Mary Lou, like she's pathetic and unworthy. I want nothing to do with her.

No! I try to shout, but only gurgle more. That's not true! My sister is *not* pathetic!

Something leaps on me again. My body thrashes side to side, but there's no pain, only a vague feeling of something rubbery pulling away from my throat. An animal snarl cuts the air above me, and the creature leaps off into the darkness once more.

My arms don't want to move. Gray creeps into the periphery of my vision. I'm... dying.

No. I don't want to die! Tammy! Anthony! Danny! I have a family. I can't leave them!

Hot tears roll down the sides of my head and gather in my ears. I refuse to give up. I'm not gonna go like this. No way. I'm only thirty-one. It's not my time.

Time.

I have only seconds left on this Earth. Images of the last days, months, and years flicker by in a slideshow. Every time Tammy smiled at me. Anthony's first word, his trying to fill in the hole Tammy dug on the beach. Tammy curling up at my side when I'd been shot, knowing I was in pain and having no other way to help but be there for me.

Great sobs roll over my brain, my body incapable of expressing them to the world.

Our wedding night, the happiest moment of my life until I held Tammy's newborn body in my arms. Danny and his best man Jeff Rodriguez hitting the champagne a little too hard and almost falling straight into our wedding cake. A flash, and I'm making love to Danny on our wedding night.

I'm a child again, playing in the woods around my parents' trailer/tent mess. How many times had I run off to be alone, to get away from my brothers? I'd grown up feeling apart from them, ignoring them so much, resenting my parents. Loving the forest. Why did I love the forest so much? I didn't know. Maybe I was a witch. Or an elf in a past life.

I've got seconds left to live, and I've wasted so many years.

Mere seconds, that I'd give anything in the world to cling to for just a little longer.

How many hours have I wished would race by at the office, bored out of my skull and wanting to go home? My mind voice laughs at the absurdity of it. How the value of time can shift so dramatically. Here, one tiny second is the most precious thing, but waiting for my wedding, I tried to make months fly away as fast as possible.

If only I could hold my children once again. To have Tammy cuddle up beside me and tell me I'm going to be okay.

The cold breeze invades my neck and goes down my throat. It shouldn't do that. I shouldn't feel the wind going inside me with my mouth closed.

Seconds left.

My last thoughts won't be fear. I won't die like that.

I picture my children smiling, refusing to think about them being told Mommy's dead. I can't do that to them.

No. I'm not going to die. I can't put my family through that. Danny needs me. Tammy and Anthony need me. I won't give up. I won't succumb. The heartbeat echoing in my head slows, barely noticeable. Nothing hurts anymore. No pain. No awareness of having a body. My mind fills in the sensation of little Tammy curling up at my side. I can't give up. I won't stop clinging to life.

I refu—

Chapter Twenty-Five
Afterlife

Vivid and bizarre images fill in the darkness.

Scenes of war with spears and primitive weapons play on the black canvas of my mind. I stand upon a stone ziggurat, surrounded by grassy plains. Men with swords clash on the steps below me, their white tunics flickering orange in the light of torches. Blood flies into the air from grotesque wounds. Each time a man cries out in anguish, the urge to laugh at his misfortune wells up within, horrifying me more at my reaction than the spectacle itself. I know the men at the base of the steps want to destroy me, but they are weak and pathetic—and they will fail.

The dream of battle swirls again into void. I'm falling backward in an endless plummet. Minutes or hours pass, I can't tell. Something glints off in the distance and falling becomes flying. A lone figure appears distinct in the murk, out jogging at night. Like a diving hawk, I fly down at myself in total silence, hovering behind as I run along the trail in Hillcrest Park. Not even the clap of sneakers on paving makes the slightest sound. The thick, confident voice of a woman with a strong accent breaks the oppressive silence.

Hello, Sssamantha.

My eyes snap open.

Beeping comes from my left. Drab white ceiling tiles blur in and out of focus above me. Something rigid squeezes my neck and presses painfully at my right shoulder. I'm aware of fabric against my arms and legs. It occurs to me the beeping keeps time with my heartbeat, though it seems a little too slow.

Holy shit, I'm alive!

I can't move my head at all, so I pivot my eyes around. The hospital room is small, and a curtain drawn around the bed blocks most of my view. A blurry figure occupies a chair to the right of the bed, but I can't keep looking in that direction due to the horrible glare in the window, like the sun is parked inches from the glass.

Feeling spreads over me as the minutes tick by. The most bizarre thing: my nerves sense individual threads in the sheets. It's too strange for words, not that I can talk, and I lose time sliding my finger side to side under the bed, mystified at the sensation. Scraps of voices drift into my awareness from outside. Dozens of people in a myriad of conversations mix with plastic crinkling, shoes squeaking, the thrum of an elevator, and the whirr of the air conditioning.

It soon becomes maddening, trying to focus on any single thread of ideas. Too many people talking all at once, like I'm back in high school in the middle of the cafeteria. A frustrated moan leaks out of my nose.

"Sam?" asks Danny, his voice rough and cracked. His chair emits a loud creaking noise as he stands. "Are you awake?"

When he leans over me, we make eye contact. He looks like he's aged ten years from the last time I'd seen him... and he stinks. Not in a horrible way, but that 'Danny smell' he's always had about him is ten times more intense, so strong it settles on my tongue like a flavor.

I try to speak, but only manage a feeble wheeze.

"Don't talk." Danny grasps my right hand in both of his, and chokes up. "The doctor said you won't be able to talk for, uhh, a while." He looks down. "There's a chance you might not be able to again."

Oh no... I blink tears out of the corners of my eyes. It doesn't matter. I can live without talking. I'm alive; that's all that matters. Or am I? Time seems to freeze still, Danny hovering over me, tears running over the stubble on his cheeks, the echoing din of the hospital corridor a meaningless haze of sound. Did I survive or is this another strange post-death dream? Could I be still lying on the road, my brain shutting down as it burns up the last traces of oxygen?

The stretched second passes.

Danny bows his head against my knuckles and weeps. "I thought I lost you, Sam. I'm so happy you're okay. Whatever your new reality is, I'll be there for you. This changes nothing between us."

I try to ask, "how bad?" but what comes out of me is just air blowing down a tube.

He sniffles back his tears and strokes my hair. "I couldn't handle it if I lost you." Again, he falls to bits and sobs on my shoulder.

Barely able to move, I lay there and absorb his grief. Why did I have to be so stupid and go jogging at night? This is my fault. All this pain on his face is my doing. What has he told the kids? As soon as I worry about them, the beeping gets faster. Tingles run up and down my limbs, the sense of coarseness in the fabric intensifies to a bed of sandpaper.

The most maddening itch imaginable spreads over my neck and right shoulder, under heavy bandages and a thick, plastic contraption that's immobilizing my skull. Wrapped in torture I can't escape from, the sheets that feel like they're flaying my skin off to the army of ten thousand fleas crawling over my throat, makes me want to scream. All I can do is blow air. Even if I could move my arms, I wouldn't be able to scratch under the brace.

A splintery *crunch* happens nearby.

"Gah! Sam!" shouts Danny.

He tries to jump back, but can't get his hand out of my grip. When I realize he's howling in pain, I let go, and he collapses back into his chair, cradling his hand. He stares at his broken finger and back to me.

"Sam?" He asks, blinking rapidly.

I try to convey apology with my facial expression.

"You broke my finger… are you in pain?"

Wheeze.

"Blink once for yes, twice for no."

I blink once.

Danny hits the call button with his left hand. "I'll get the nurse or someone to give you a shot or something."

My gaze turns downward, guilty. The flare up of sensation fades, leaving the sheets normal but the itching is still driving me crazy.

"A couple out jogging found you." He lets off a manic laugh. "Who the hell goes jogging at midnight?"

I force a cheesy smile. Sorry for being dumb.

"They think a coyote attacked you. Maybe a pack of them. One doctor even said a wolf." Danny's eyes dart, looking a bit crazed. "A wolf. Wolf, can you believe that? Here in Orange County."

No… it was a man. That moment comes back to my thoughts, and in the prescience of calm, I recall the pressure of human fingers digging into my shoulder and side. As I ran, a man had lifted me off my feet and hurled me thirty feet into the trees. I'm sure of it now. How is that even possible? Yet, I remember it like it happened two seconds ago. Not a coyote. Not a wolf. I blink twice, but Danny doesn't notice.

He grasps my wrist with his left hand, likely wary of having another finger broken. "You lost so much blood they were telling me to prepare for bad news. Oh, God, Sam, I'm so glad you're still here."

That makes two of us, I think. I don't care if I'm a mute invalid in a wheelchair for the rest of my life. At least I'm here.

"They've got you on IV antibiotics for infection. You had a real big wound, and there's a massive amount of stitches."

I look up at Danny, but cringe away from the nuclear furnace the window has become. The glow is so bright it's painful to my eyes. Guess they've got me loaded up on the good shit. Probably why I'm not crippled with agony. Oddly enough, other than the infuriating itch, my body doesn't hurt much.

Clattering goes by in the corridor and the fragrance of turkey and gravy washes over me. The instant my brain processes the smell, nausea churns inside me. Merely thinking about eating pushes me to the edge of vomiting.

Danny grips my arm and shoulder as I convulse. "Sam? What's wrong?"

I gurgle.

"You need to throw up?"

One blink.

A nurse walks in as he cranks the bed up so I'm

in a sitting position. "You hit the call button?" she asks.

My eyes water from her perfume. Fire fills my sinuses like I insufflated half a bottle of it. The brace keeps me from cringing away. Oh, if there's a Hell, this is it. Maybe I really *did* die.

"My wife's in pain. Is there something you can give her?"

The nurse looks over a chart hanging from the end of the bed and shakes her head. "Not without a doctor being involved. She's already on a pain drip. A fairly high dose, too. She shouldn't be feeling much of anything. In fact, I'm surprised she's even awake. She shouldn't be lucid."

I stare at her.

"Mrs. Moon, are you aware you're in a hospital?" asks the nurse.

"She can't talk," says Danny, a hint of confrontation in his tone.

Damn this brace. Even if my muscles remained on speaking terms with me, I can't nod with my neck locked in plastic. I do manage a thumbs up with my right hand. Well, that's something.

The nurse steps closer and examines my eyes. "Do you recognize the man standing beside you?"

Again, I give a thumbs up.

She does the 'track my fingers with your eyes' thing. Evidently, I pass the test, which surprises her. When she asks my age, I hold up three fingers, then one. After that, she runs off to get a notepad and pen.

When she returns, she places the pad of paper under my hand and sticks the pen in my grip. She asks, "How do you feel?"

I write 'itch like hell,' and below it, 'smelling food makes me sick.'

The nurse gawks at the pad. "I really don't understand how she's so coherent on that much painkiller. We had a guy a couple months ago on a slightly lower dose. The doctor asked him who the president was and he said 'purple.'"

Danny chuckles.

Another whiff of food goes by, and I nearly gag.

"Oh, don't worry about that." The nurse fusses at my neck brace. "You're in no condition for solid food, Mrs. Moon. It'll be some time before you have to worry about eating. For the time being, you're on IV nutrition. I suspect you'll be on a liquid diet for a while. At least until we see how your injuries heal."

Small blessings. Concentrating on the idea that I won't have to eat that turkey helps me avoid choking on bile. I look at Danny, then write, "Sorry for being stupid and going out at night alone."

"Sam…" Danny brushes my hair off my face. "Don't talk like that. You're no helpless dame."

Hah. Maybe I wasn't before, but I am now. I can't *not* laugh at the thought, even though my laughing is only a toneless oscillation of air. Wow, that hurt.

"Easy." Danny pats my forehead. "Don't try to talk. Give yourself time to heal."

I write, "Did my spine break? Am I going to walk again?"

"There's nothing on your chart about a spinal injury," says the nurse, glancing at the pad. "If you're having difficulty moving, it might be an aftereffect of the surgical anesthesia, but that's somewhat worrying considering it's been two days since you got out of the OR."

Two days!? I rapidly scribble, "Danny! How are the kids? What did you tell them?"

"They know you got hurt and you're in the hospital. They're staying with Mary Lou right now. Tammy's demanding to come see you but she's too little. The hospital won't let children younger than six in to visit."

Grr.

"Nurse?" asks Danny, holding up his right hand, with an obviously broken pinky and ring finger. "Since I'm already at the hospital… think someone can take a look at this?"

"Oh, ouch. Of course. Come with me."

Danny leans down and kisses me on the head. "I'll be back as soon as I can. Try to get some rest."

Yeah. I don't think the flea army chowing down on my neck and shoulder is going to permit that. I write, "Okay. Sorry about your finger."

The nurse leads Danny out of my room, and I am once again alone with my thoughts. I guess Chad was right. After being shot at twice in a month, my guardian angel must've gotten drunk and fallen asleep on me when I went jogging.

Hah. Guardian angels indeed. How do people come up with this stuff?

Chapter Twenty-Six
Innocent Victims

Soon after Danny leaves with the nurse, a heavy, groggy sensation spreads over my mind.

The next thing I know, it's dark out. Danny's still in the chair at my bedside, his face lit pale in the harsh glow of his Kindle. The itching hasn't let up, and I'm astounded that I managed to fall asleep with it. Danny's e-reader is enough to illuminate my whole room. Wow... what a screen on that thing. The door's pushed nearly closed, muting the sounds of activity outside as well as the light from the hallway. My monitor's gone, which explains the lack of beeping.

Danny's scent rides heavy on each breath. I swallow out of reflex; my mouth and throat are dry. Not painfully so, but it's unnerving that the usual saliva isn't there. Maybe the attack did something or the drugs I'm on right now are playing havoc with my system.

"Hey." Danny perks up. "You slept all day."

Guess I did.

He shuts off the Kindle, making the room darker but not so much I can't see, and approaches the bed, again taking my hand. I'm not the only Moon sporting a rigid brace now. His two broken fingers are wrapped together to an aluminum strut to keep them immobile. The sight of his bandage fills me with remorse. What happened to me doesn't matter at all by comparison, because *I* did that to him.

"Some of your people came by this afternoon, including Chad, but you slept straight through their visit. They'll come back tomorrow."

I try to nod, but this infernal goddamned contraption locked around my neck won't let me. Danny looks like crap. He gets the idea when I squirm at my hand, and lets go so I can write.

"You look fried. Have you been sleeping in that chair for two days?"

"Yeah. I couldn't leave you." His voice breaks up a bit as tears well at the corners of his eyes. "I thought at any minute, you could…" He swallows hard. "I wanted to be there for every moment you had left."

Guilt settles like a lead weight in my chest, though I make myself smile while writing, "You're not getting rid of me that easy."

He laughs, wiping his eyes. "How you feeling?"

"I feel okay," I write. "But damn this itches. If you want to sleep home tonight, it's okay. You look sicker than I feel." I point a finger at where the monitor used to be, and keep writing, "I guess I'm okay if they took away the beepy thing."

"You got a bad one I think. The machine kept alarming all day long like your heart stopped or you were going into cardiac arrest. After the sixth false alarm, they took it out. Guess they never got around to bringing in a new one."

"Oh," I write. "Please call Mary Lou and let her know how I'm doing."

He nods before looking himself over. "Ugh. I've been in the same clothes for days. Maybe I should go clean up."

I don't tell him his scent is overpowering. "Okay."

Danny leans down and kisses me lightly on the lips. The warmth of his face against mine stirs an odd feeling of... hunger inside me. And not in the sensual way. It's freaky enough that I can only stare at him. "I'll be back in the morning," he says. "Make that late morning. I want to stop by your sister's and check on the kids, let them know their mother's doing better."

"When can I go home?" I write.

He grimaces. "Last thing the doctor said made it sound like at least... two months."

Ugh! Two months in this torture contraption is going to give me nightmares for the rest of my life.

"I know, I know." Danny reacts to the face I make. "You're tough though, Sam. I bet you'll be out in one."

Heh. I smile.

Danny kisses me once more and walks out in a slow trudge, his suit jacket hung over his back on one finger at his shoulder. He doesn't really want to leave, but he needs a proper night's sleep. When he hesitates at the door and looks back at me, I smile at him and (since I still can't move) give him a thumbs up.

"See you soon." Danny bows his head, sighs, and walks out of sight.

Drifting back and forth from restless to guilty, I stare at the ceiling as the attack replays in my thoughts. Why did I have to go jogging that night? I should've stayed home, safe inside, so Danny wouldn't have had to go through thinking he'd lost me. No matter how many times he says it, I don't think I'll ever forgive myself for doing that to him. My arm curls at my side, cradling an imaginary Tammy. That gets me fuming that the hospital won't let her in to see me.

Some time of staring at the ceiling later, I manage to reach the TV remote on the night table to my right and flick the set on. My left arm has decided to rejoin me, and much to my relief, my legs are once again under my control. If not for the three IV lines tethering me, I'd even try to walk. Oh, wait a minute, they're on a wheeled post. I could probably go to the bathroom if need be, though I lack the urge.

What have I been doing for two days? I slide my hand under the blanket, checking for a diaper, and find a catheter. Oh, ouch! *That's* uncomfortable. So much for needing to get out of bed.

Hours of mindless TV go by. As 6:00 a.m. approaches, grogginess sets in, and I let my eyes flutter closed.

I snap awake to a painfully bright room. Chad, Montoya, Anders, and Rivera crowd around my bed. They're in the midst of a conversation about me being asleep *again* in the middle of the day, which worries them that I might be in worse shape than anyone's let on.

"Hey," I rasp. Wow, did I just talk?

They all startle and look down at me.

"Mooney!" yells Chad. "Holy shit, it's good to see you awake."

"Hey, Sam," says Michelle Rivera. "Looks like you had a rough week."

"Yeah." My voice is rough and wheezy, but present.

"You probably shouldn't be talking too much yet." Chad pats my left arm. "We interviewed the couple who found you. They didn't see anything or anyone else out there. Fullerton Police are looking into it as well, but they're baffled. Did the attack happen in Hillcrest Park? You lost a major amount of blood but they didn't find much at the scene."

"The detective thinks you were attacked somewhere else and dumped," says Montoya.

"No. In park," I rasp. "Something... hit from behind." I wave my hand around in a circle. "Flew into a tree."

"They're at a loss for a motive too." Chad sits on the edge of the bed. "Nothing was taken. Even your gun was still there. There's no evidence of any sexual assault."

Michelle shudders. "Could be some 'rando' serial killer. Hit you with his car and tried to finish things with a knife."

"Gang?" I shift my gaze among my team. "Revenge?"

"Doesn't seem like it. FBI says they got 'em all." Chad shakes his head. "Guess your guardian angel was off at O'Hara's getting drunk."

I fight the urge to chuckle. "Chad, you know I don't believe in that stuff." I swallow and take a couple quick, labored breaths that feel strange, like I'm overinflating my lungs. "Those assholes tried to kill me again, and they almost succeeded."

"They're blaming coyotes," says Montoya.

"No. Not animals. A man." I reach up as if cradling a dangling amulet. "He had a medallion around his neck. I saw it right in front of my face. Round... gold with rubies."

Chad shakes his head. "The police didn't find any other footprints in the dirt. It couldn't have been a person unless they were doing some *Mission Impossible* shit with rope, hanging over you."

Montoya and Rivera chuckle.

"Neck wound, lot of blood loss but little found at the scene," says Bryce Anders. "Maybe you got attacked by a vampire?"

Chad rolls his eyes, as do I.

Michelle swats him in the arm. "Come on, Anders. Be serious."

"I am." He holds up his hands. "Not saying a *literal* vampire. Some freako that thinks he's one. There have been a couple dozen attacks like this over the past few years. Cops still haven't found a suspect."

Montoya puts his hands on his hips, frowning at the floor. "If that's true, why isn't it on the news? You'd think something like that would've gone nuts... Serial killers become media sensations. Remember that one in New York in the 70s? The whole thing was a furor."

"Sorry, Ernie. I wasn't alive back then." Bryce winks. "I dunno why they're keeping it quiet. That detective mentioned the previous similar cases. But he didn't think Moon got attacked by the same person or group since she's alive."

"Oh, Sam." Chad grins. "You're in the paper. Set off a coyote panic. People are calling for a hunt to thin their numbers before they attack some kid."

"No. Wasn't coyotes. Don't let them kill animals because of me." I stare down at myself under the sheet. I don't need even *more* guilt on my head. Those poor creatures had nothing to do with this. "I'm sure it was a man. Please stop them from murdering coyotes. They're innocent."

"Prosecutor's going after Brauerman with 94 counts. We found a few more in his computer that weren't on the phone records you got. He's looking at serious time if he's convicted," says Chad. "It might wind up being pled out."

"Okay. What about Donnie Vento?" I ask.

"I hear they offered to go easier on Brauerman if he testified against Vento. He agreed, but couldn't pick the guy's photo correctly, and there's no evidence we could find that shows the two ever met. Looks like Donnie was just a disaster as a HUD agent without being a criminal on top of it."

"Oh well." I shrug. "It was just a theory."

Chad squeezes my shoulder. "Don't worry about it for now. There'll be plenty more investigations for you once you're out of that hospital bed. Michelle's already collecting money for cake and shit when you come back to the office."

She grins.

Thinking of cake doesn't instantly nauseate me, so maybe I *am* feeling better. "That's sweet of you guys. I'm not sure how long I'll be out, but I'll be back as soon as I can." My eyes half-lid.

"You look beat." Chad stands, making the bed jostle. "Guess we'll let you get some rest. We gotta get back to the office anyway before Nico throws a fit."

"All right. Thanks for visiting, you guys."

One by one, they grasp my hand and file out.

Alone again, I feel myself falling back to sleep. At some point in the vagary of time, I become remotely aware of Danny speaking to me, but whatever he said distorts in my foggy brain to unintelligible sound.

***

My eyes open to a dark room.

The clock on the bedside table reads 9:28 p.m. I'm wide awake, and ravenous, but I've still got the IV drip feeding me. Guess I suffer an empty stomach. Danny's gone, but he's propped a dry-erase board in his chair with a note that Jeff begged him for help with a case, and it's a 'make or break the whole firm' kind of big deal. He promises to be back tomorrow as soon as he wakes up.

I cringe at the constant, infuriating itch. The army of fleas has multiplied. It feels like half a million biting bugs have gotten in under the bandages and brace, devouring my flesh in an unending cascade of teeny-tiny bites. Fidgeting at the rigid plastic doesn't help, and I can't get my fingers under it. With a huff, I glare at the ceiling, fuming with anger at my present situation. I'd give anything to make this itching stop!

Blackness creeps in at the edges of my vision. My limbs go leaden once again, and it feels like I'm sliding backward down a long inky hallway. A mental scream floods my thoughts. I sit up in shock, stark naked and curled up on the floor of a tiny cube-shaped room of solid onyx. The glassy floor is cold to my bare skin. There are no doors or windows—or any light source, but I can see.

I grasp my throat, feeling smooth, intact skin. No bumps or scars, or gaping wounds. The wall I'm huddled against is shiny enough to serve as a mirror. Other than pallid, my body is perfect. Oh, this is some new freaky level of dream. Locked in a little prison cell naked. I know they do that with mental patients or when they throw a prisoner in punitive solitary, they sometimes take all their clothes so they don't hang or strangle themselves.

But... why? I've never even gotten a parking ticket.

I sit there in a ball, hugging my knees to my chest, mortified despite being aware I'm dreaming. Onyx prison cells with no doors don't exist. This *has* to be in my mind. I keep my head down, hiding behind my long hair.

After what feels like hours, a feeling of lightness comes over me, and my body rises into the air, uncurling to hang limp. My head lolls back, arms draped to the sides, my chest leading the way as I float toward the ceiling.

Instead of pressing into freezing glass-smooth stone, I pass through into a cloud of dark smoke, and the ceiling of my hospital room emerges from the billowing mass. The soft texture of the bed and my gown wraps me in the warm reassurance that I had, in fact, been dreaming of solitary confinement.

A tickle runs down my chin. I grab at it, reflexively trying to kill the bug. Instead of smashed insect on my fingers, I stare at a smear of blood. Oh, shit. Did I hurt myself somehow in my sleep? I swipe a tissue from the nightstand box and dab at my face. Fortunately, there's not much. By the third tissue, there's no trace of blood.

Whew. Maybe I had a nosebleed.

People run by outside in a panic, voices chattering about someone coding. I hate hospitals. There's so much death here. Again, I flick on the television, hoping to drown out the voices in the hallway. Absentmindedly, I trace my fingers around my stomach, noting that I no longer feel like I could eat a whole cow. Guess my brain caught up to the rest of my body telling it that I'm getting nutrition from a needle.

Speaking of which, I'm acutely aware of three slivers of metal jabbed in my arm from the IVs. I wouldn't call them painful, but they're almost as irritating as the itching I can't scratch. Great, another small misery.

I'm not paralyzed, or even mute. Despite my current discomfort, I smile to myself, daydreaming about how awesome it will feel when Tammy and Anthony run into my arms. Having to wait a month or two for that moment is worse than anything else.

But hey, at least I'm alive.

Chapter Twenty-Seven
A Couple Days

Fullerton detectives show up late the next afternoon and take my statement regarding the attack. Being half-awake and having a heap of trouble concentrating on anything, I get hung up on the whole coyote thing and keep repeating that the animals are innocent. The cops think I'm medicated and loopy, so they start talking slower. To my utter lack of surprise, they have no suspects.

Danny shows up at one in the afternoon. His arrival stirs me out of my shockingly deep sleep. We talk about the kids and Mary Lou for a while. It breaks my heart when he hands me a get well card that the kids made for me, while telling me that Tammy asks every day if 'Mommy's coming home tomorrow.'

"Did you hear about the old guy at the end of the hall?" asks Danny.

I shift my eyes to look at him. Another day or
two in this brace and I'm going to rip it off myself.
"No... what happened? I heard a commotion, but no
one's said anything."

"This old man six rooms down the hall from
here almost died. They found blood all over his
pillow. Someone stabbed him in the neck with like
an icepick or something and let him bleed out."

I gasp. "That's horrible!"

"If he wasn't already *in* a hospital, he wouldn't
have made it. They say he lost a lot of blood. Too
much to survive, but a transfusion saved him. Then
he had a heart attack, but they brought him back
from that with those paddle things."

"Poor bastard. Is he okay?"

Danny nods. "Amazingly enough, yeah. The
guy's over eighty."

I can't help but harbor a little guilt that I'm
feeling much better. Even the itching has stopped.

Staying awake, however, proves close to
impossible. Day falls away to night, at which point
my eyes pop open again and won't close. Danny's
asleep in the chair beside my bed. He stirs a few
hours later and goes to the bathroom. When he
returns, we talk on and off for a while about a case
he's working. He complains about how obnoxious
his client is, like this woman insists on carrying her
micro-dog everywhere. Even thinks she's taking it
into the courtroom for the lawsuit.

I laugh.

Danny smiles at me. "You look great, Sam. You

don't even sound like anything happened."

"Awesome. Maybe I can go home then. Or at least get this medieval thing off my neck."

He yawns and starts discussing Tammy's imminent start at preschool, but he zonks out again in mid-sentence. I can't remember ever being this awake at two in the morning before, even during college. They say messed up things can happen to a person after trauma. One dude woke up from a coma speaking Russian without explanation. At least I'm still using English.

I pass a few hours channel flipping the absolutely awful things on TV in the early morning. Grogginess hits me soon after the sky outside begins to show signs of approaching day. Before I pass out, a different nurse breezes into the room with a pushcart, singing softly to herself in Spanish. She's middle-aged, probably shorter than me, and on the heavy side.

"Good morning, Mrs. Moon," says the nurse. "Sorry to bother you so early, but it's time to change your dressing."

"Can I get Thousand Island this time?"

She laughs.

Danny stirs, sits up, and yawns.

"Okay, I need to ask you not to move much once I take the brace open, all right?"

I stare at the nurse. "How much longer do I have to wear this contraption?"

"Until the doctor says it's okay. If you move too much, you make the wound angry and it will take

265

longer to heal."

"Right." I sigh at the ceiling.

It takes the woman a few minutes to open screws and clamps, and peel the two halves of heavy plastic away. The rush of cool air on my skin feels amazing.

"*Ay Dios Mio!*" cries the nurse.

"What?" I look up at her.

She stares in shock at me for a second or two before rushing out the door with the brace in hand, calling for a doctor.

I try not to move my head and shift my gaze to the right, at Danny. "Please tell me I haven't like grown another eyeball in my neck or something."

Danny stands and hurries over, leaning on the bed. "Holy shit, Sam…" His fingers brush my shoulder at the base of my neck, and he holds up black thread. "I… all the stitches are out… the thread's just sitting on top of your skin. There's a long, jagged mark where they closed the wound, but it's sealed up."

Neat. "Wow. Guess that's why it's not itching anymore."

"Uhh, Sam." He caresses my throat with the backs of his fingers. "Does this hurt?"

"No. It feels wonderful. Keep that up and we're going to get started on baby number three."

Most of the color drains from Danny's face. "There are a lot of red and purple and bruises around it. Are you sure it doesn't hurt?"

"Positive." I sit up and grab my neck. "What the

fuck?"

"That's one way to put it." Danny keeps staring at me.

I squeeze and poke at myself, but it doesn't hurt at all. That night, I distinctly remember feeling like the inside of my throat had been exposed to the wind, but I have no explanation for how in the hell *this* happened.

"Check my back…" I pull the hospital gown up, exposing myself to Danny. I hit that tree hard. If not my spine, I had to break at least some ribs. "Any bruising there?"

His hand, fiery and warm, presses against my skin, right below the shoulder blade. "No. You look amazing, but you're a little cold."

Rapid Spanish approaches outside. I hastily pull the gown back into place as the same nurse enters, all but shoving a Middle Eastern man toward me. He's early thirties, thick, black hair, and on the fairly handsome end of nerdy.

"Mrs. Moon? I'm Doctor Shah. Nurse Guererra here asked me to have a look at you."

"Is this going to involve full frontal nudity or just morphine?" I ask, wondering if he's going to be invasive or just give me more pain meds.

He chuckles. "Good to see your sense of humor is intact. Might I?"

"Knock yourself out." I lay back and let the hospital gown drop off my shoulders. He's a doctor. He's seen so many boobs he's probably not even excited by them anymore.

"Oh, my word." He examines my neck and shoulder, prodding with his finger. "The injury looks like it's been on the mend for about a month. Does it hurt when I press down?"

"No."

We repeat this exchange about ten times, until I finally reply, "A little," when he jabs his finger in hard. Even if I hadn't been torn open, that prod would've been mildly painful. He's mystified at the stitches having emerged from my skin, still caked with scabbed blood every quarter inch.

"Mrs. Moon, your recovery has progressed remarkably well. Unbelievably, in fact. Are you experiencing anything unusual?"

"I'm a little groggy, and I'd appreciate it if you could turn down the sun a little."

"It's painful to look at?"

"Yeah." I nod.

At the doctor's gesture, Nurse Guererra hurries over to the window and draws the blinds. He spends a few minutes listening to my heartbeat. I lucked out. This is the first time in my life I had a doctor who didn't keep his stethoscope in the freezer before the exam. It's not icy against my skin.

"Your chart indicates you showed signs of bradycardia. The beat's still on the slow side, but it's sped up to the slow end of normal."

"That's good, right?"

"Quite." He grasps my throat in both hands, applying light pressure at several points before leaning back. "Everything feels structurally sound, not even any inflammation of your lymph nodes. I've never seen anything like this before. The only explanation that makes any sense to me is some kind of massive error of documentation. Your injuries couldn't have been as severe as indicated upon your admission. It's astounding that you're even able to speak at all, much less mere days later."

"It was dark. Guess I looked worse than I was."

Danny fidgets.

Doctor Shah scratches his head. "I'm at a loss, Mrs. Moon. You appear to be perfectly healthy. If you don't mind, I'd like to run an MRI just to double check. If that comes back clean, I don't see any need to keep you here. You should be able to get by with a basic wound dressing for a week or so. You'll need to keep it dry, and your husband can redress it once a day. We'll make sure he knows how to do that before you leave."

I grin like a little kid offered cake. "Awesome. I'm dying to get home and be with my kids. No more brace, right?"

"Nope. Doesn't seem to be any need for it now."

"Wonderful. Those things violate the Geneva Convention." I roll my head around, enjoying the ability to move my neck.

"We'll be back in a little while to bring you to the MRI room," says the doctor.

"Great. Oh…" I glance at the tube going over my thigh. "Any chance of getting this thing unplugged from my… yeah?"

Doctor Shah nods to the nurse. "I don't see why not. You certainly don't seem bedridden. Nurse Guererra will help with that. Let me go set up the scan."

The woman glances at the collection bag hanging on the side of the bed and gives me a furtive look of alarm. Once the doctor leaves, she pulls the curtain closed around the bed, lifts my gown, and removes the catheter. Now *there's* a sensation I never want to experience again. When she gathers the tubing and the bag, my jaw almost drops open. It's got a small quantity of urine, about what I'd expect from peeing once. I'd been out cold for two days and lying here for two more…

No wonder she's freaked out. That *is* a little disturbing.

Danny runs his hand over my neck and shoulder, still with a dumbstruck look on his face. "Umm. I guess we shouldn't ask questions, but be grateful."

"Works for me." I sink back against the pillow. My bones are heavy. All I want to do at the moment is close my eyes and sleep.

His uneasy expression flickers into a grin. "You're one tough girl. I bet you'll be back to work in a couple of days." He pulls me into his arms, hugging me like I'd be gone forever if he let go.

Overwhelmed, I clamp on, sniffling into his shoulder. Maybe I should think about changing jobs, doing something where I have *zero* chance of being shot at. The memory of lying there, gazing into the stars and thinking my remaining time on this Earth amounted to mere seconds makes me cling for dear life. All those moments that I almost lost: the kids' first days at school; first time on a bike; sports or ballet or whatever they get into; their first dates… everything I came so close to not being a part of hits me hard. I wind up bawling and stammering apology after apology.

"Hey, hey… Sam." Danny rocks me side to side. "Stop crying. It's not your fault."

"I shouldn't have gone out at night like that." I shudder with grief at what nearly happened. One thing is clear to me now—nothing matters more than my family. Not my job, not money, not even crime. I don't know how I got this chance, but every waking second I have left is precious.

Danny eases me back down in bed, and sits there a while stroking my hair and smiling at me. He's crying too, out of joy. Oh, God, how reckless was I to do that to him? The next thing I know, Danny's nudging my shoulder. Cloth tight against my neck tells me there's a bandage over the wound I hadn't had before.

"Huh what?" I squint at the painfully bright room, raising an arm to shield my eyes.

He hands me a log of aluminum foil that smells of eggs. Okay, a small burrito. He's got one for himself, and peels it open after sitting in the chair beside me.

"Should I eat? What about the scan?"

"They did that already. You slept through it. The doctor's a little concerned with your grogginess, but it could be from all the painkillers you've been hopped up on."

I open the egg burrito and take a bite. Ack. Hospital food sucks. I've had better tasting plastic. It's off-putting, but I force myself to eat about half of it before I can't take any more. The warm egg-cheese-bread mass sits in my gut like a bowling ball in a bucket of acid. Ugh. What's the phrase? 'Mistakes were made?'

"Sam?" asks Danny. "You okay?"

"Yeah. I don't think the stomach was quite ready for solid food. Either that or they scraped that off the road."

He chuckles, holding his own up. "Mine's all right."

I hand him the remainder. "Go on. Don't waste it. I'm done. Maybe I'll have some toast later."

Danny leans closer, taking the burrito. "You feeling sick or feverish?"

"No, just… nauseated." I lie back and close my eyes again, listening to my stomach groan and complain.

"Mr. Moon?" asks a woman by the door. "The doctor has sent over the discharge paperwork. If your wife is ready to go home, we just need a couple signatures."

"Rock on." I do a fist pump.

"Okay," mumbles Danny around my half-burrito. "Be right there."

He inhales the last of the breakfast, gives my hand a squeeze, and walks out after the woman in the gray skirt suit. The storm in my gut brews stronger. Only the burn of IV needles outdoes it for discomfort. Sick and tired of the jabbing heat in my arm, I snarl, sit up, and yank the IV lines out, tape and all, barely noticing any pain.

A little trail of blood runs down my arm. Mesmerized by the cherry red against the vanilla white of my skin, I stare, unable to take my eyes off it—until the small hole closes before my eyes.

What? My fingertips probe the area, which isn't even tender anymore. No hole, no trace that a needle had ever been there before. Oh, this is too weird.

My stomach churns, boiling over.

Shit!

I leap out of bed on sluggish, unresponsive legs, and wobble into the bathroom, collapsing on my knees in front of the toilet. My body lurches once, then again, and the third time I heave, the contents of my stomach splatter all over the bowl. I convulse over and over, my body in full on mutiny that I dared subject it to those disastrous eggs. There's nothing left inside me to come out, but I can't stop gagging. It's almost as if my body is pissed off and trying to punish me.

Right as I expect to see my intestines come flying out of my mouth, the convulsions subside, leaving me draped over the toilet and gasping. Surprisingly, I'm not dripping with sweat even though I ought to be. My heart races, the roar of blood rushing through my head becomes deafening. The smell of the eggs below my nose causes me to heave again.

I recoil from the toilet and avert my face. Yeah, it'll be a while before I can go anywhere near eggs again. After wiping my face and flushing the toilet, I stagger back to bed with a hand over my wounded gut. Feels like I went three rounds with Chad in an MMA fight and he kept kicking me there.

With a groan, I flop on the bed. Shit. I don't have any clothes here. They probably cut them off me in the operating room. Screw it. I want to go home so bad I don't care if I have to wear a hospital gown out the door.

Chapter Twenty-Eight
Setting Sunshine

Neither Danny nor the nurse are amused at my declaration that I'll go naked when they inform us that we can't take the hospital gown out of the building. Begrudgingly, I wait in the room while Danny runs home to get me something to wear. Again, I wind up passing out so it feels like his absence went by in seconds. I change into jeans, a t-shirt, and sneakers, and suffer the mandatory wheelchair to the hospital's sliding glass doors.

In the short trip from the exit to the curved loading zone where Danny's BMW waits, both my arms develop a nasty, painful sunburn. I've never burned like that before, though I didn't really ever tan despite my fondness for sunbathing. I'd either get a little darker, or hit lobster red. But feeling like someone lit me on fire is new.

I dive into the car and cringe away from the

sunlight slanting across the seat. By the time Danny gets in, the redness has faded, though I'm still sore. Complaining about that will get me stuck back in the hospital, so I keep my trap shut.

The ride home is a constant, irritating battle trying to keep myself out of the shifting patches of sun, which burn like hell. Danny notices me fidgeting, but doesn't say a word. Twenty something minutes after leaving the hospital, we roll up into our driveway next to my momvan.

I eye the run from the car to the front door and dislike my unattached garage even more.

"Once you're situated, I'm going to pick the kids up." Danny glances sideways at me when I don't move. "Is something wrong?"

I fidget. "I want to stay out of the sun. I think I'm having some kind of reaction from the meds."

"Well, you *have* been kind of light-averse since you woke up. You're even squinting now."

"You know how when the eye doctor puts those dilation drops in, it's too painful to look at the world without sunglasses?"

"Right?"

"Yeah, well that's me right now."

"Hmm." Danny puts it in park. "I could get an umbrella?"

"It's okay. I can manage it." I take a deep breath, brace myself, and fling the door open. It feels like I'm roasting alive as I sprint from the car to the front door and practically dive into the comfort of the dim house. As soon as I'm out of the sun, my body relaxes.

Danny jogs up to the door, leaning in and staring at me. "Sam? Are you sure you're okay?"

I turn away so he can't see the red marks on my hands and arms. "Yeah. I'm fine. Please hurry up and bring the kids home. I'm dying to see them!"

"Sure thing, babe." He pats the doorjamb twice. "Are you sure you don't need me to help you up to bed?"

"Yeah, I'm good." I don't move except to peer over my shoulder at him. Hopefully, my face isn't as red as it feels.

Danny gives me the strangest look as he backs out, like he's trying to figure out what kind of new, bizarre circumstance we're trapped in. I dunno. Maybe I'm pregnant or something and this sun allergy will go away.

After a wave, I head inside and to the bedroom. Nothing makes me feel funky like spending almost a week in the same hospital gown and bed without hot water and soap being part of my routine. I want to shower, but the doctor told me not to get the wound wet. I run a bath and climb in, careful to keep water from going above my breasts. Despite being desperate for a shampoo, I begrudgingly content myself with a soak and some delicate washcloth maneuvering around my face. Not long after I'm dried and on the couch, Danny pulls back in.

A screaming Tammy runs in the front door and leaps onto me. Anthony, in the much less steady gait of a two-year-old, arrives soon after, and shimmies up to sit beside me. Tammy's beyond distraught, wailing and clinging like she'd thought I'd died. I gather them both in my arms, rocking them side to side while muttering apologies for being away so long.

Maybe ten minutes later, my daughter collects herself to stare up at me.

"I'm sorry, Tam Tam. I'll never scare you like that again."

"The man said you weren't coming back," says Tammy.

Danny drops his keys.

"What?" I ask. "What man?"

"The tall man. He woke me up when you got hurt and said he was sorry for making a mistake, and you were gonna go away f'ever." She sniffles into sobbing again.

"I'm never going away, sweetie." I heft Anthony up a little higher on my left, and hug them both. "I'd move Heaven and Earth for you both, and I won't let anything hurt you. Even if the Devil himself tried to take you, I'd punch him in his pointy nose."

The kids giggle.

"I thought you didn't believe in that stuff," says Danny, edging up behind the couch.

Feels like I should be crying from joy at the moment, but no tears flow. "I don't. It's just a figure of speech."

"You look tired, hon," says Danny.

"Yeah, I am. I guess miraculous healing takes a lot out of a girl."

His expression goes strained.

Whatever happened, I'm sure it's nothing we won't be able to cope with.

***

I rattle around the house all night, wide awake.

It feels like someone's standing right behind me... a woman, whispering in my ear. Whenever I turn though, I find myself alone. Unable to sleep, I get out of bed to avoid disturbing Danny. Standing in the front window, I listen to the neighbors across the street screwing. We don't know them well, and they've never gone at it this loud before... but I suppose I don't usually stand in our front window after one in the morning very often. The refrigerator kicks on, ratting and whirring. It's got a grinding sound in the mechanism that hadn't been there before. Ugh. Money's tight already. Having to replace a major appliance is going to hurt. I think I'm going to let it limp along until it drops dead.

Fine flecks on the glass stand out in sharp contrast to the night lawn. I'm a little behind on cleaning apparently. The grass catches my eye in a captivating display of wavering. Each individual blade glows in the moonlight, rendered in exquisite detail, even the ridges. Oh, that's too weird. How am I seeing that from here?

Hunger swirls in my gut. I skipped dinner,

nauseated at the smell of Danny's pot roast. Not that he screwed it up, but I'm sick or something. The drugs are still in my system. Maybe tomorrow I'll experiment with chicken soup.

TV kills some time. I don't feel tired at all until close to 5:30 a.m., when I drag myself through the house and crawl into bed.

***

Unpleasant warmth nudges me awake.

The bedroom is painfully bright, even with my eyes closed. Anthony prattles along with Barney. Confused at why he'd be watching it in our bedroom, I force my eyelids open and sit up. But our bedroom TV is off; the sound's coming from the hallway, as clear as if I stood in the room with it.

I don't hear Tammy, but was today her first day at preschool? Oh, no! I curl up and struggle not to cry. I missed her first day of school! Did she run in there all smiles or did she flip out and refuse to go? From the stories I heard, Mary Lou had been the latter, clinging to Mom on her first day of kindergarten and shrieking, begging not to be abandoned. Our parents hadn't bothered with preschool. In fact, Mary Lou had such a fit, they tried homeschooling the boys for a while, but being the slackers they were, eventually, they were ordered to send my brothers to a real school. By the time I came around, they'd given up on the homeschool thing. Mary Lou told me I didn't seem happy about going, but I didn't throw a fit either. Like the nurse who has to change the bedpan of an elderly patient, I scrunched up my face and dealt with it.

Shit. Sorrow turns to anger at myself for sleeping through that, and a bit at Danny for *letting* me sleep through that. I sit up, ready to bite his head off, but my fury sputters out when Tammy giggles. I stare at the clock. Oh, right. It's only the second week of August. She doesn't start preschool until next week.

Whew. I flop on by back, relieved, staring at the ceiling.

"Hey, Jeff," says Danny, like he's standing next to me. "Yeah, it's me. I'm at home. Sam's still not ready to be alone, so I'll be working from here for a couple days."

Jeff Rodriguez murmurs.

"Yeah, absolutely. If that happens, I'll ask her sister to come by and be with her, but unless things are on fire, I want to be here for her."

Aww. Warmth spreads over my chest at hearing that. I am so damn lucky. Maybe there *is* something to that guardian angel thing. Who gets hit by a car, flung into a tree, has their throat cut open, and winds up home feeling fine days later? Some questions will devour the mind and aren't even worth considering. At least, for now.

Shying away from the furnace of a window, I scoot across the bed to Danny's side and get to my feet. My muscles protest every motion, reducing my attempt to walk to the bathroom into a drunken stagger. That's what I get for staying up all damn night. Like a zombie, I shamble into the bathroom, hike up my nightgown, and sit on the toilet.

After a few minutes of nothing, I tap my foot on the rug. "Any day now…"

Well, this is alarming. Doesn't feel like I have to go, but I can't remember the last time I peed. The heaviness in my limbs increases, making me feel welded to the toilet. Ugh. Is this fatigue normal? Maybe when they gave me that transfusion, they used stale blood or something. Sitting there in total silence, my senses hone in on my heartbeat. Each pulse happens slower and slower, with a feeling like a fist pressed against my breastbone. I shiver with panic when I can count to ten between beats.

I shouldn't be alive.

But I don't feel in great distress. Groggy yeah, but in the midst of cardiac failure? No.

Twenty seconds pass between beats. I count to twenty again, and another squidgy compression follows. One beat every twenty seconds is *not* normal. My hands look so pale, I can't believe what my eyes are telling me. Come on, Sam. Wake up. This has to be another dream like that black prison cell. There's no way I'm sitting here alive with a pulse this sluggish.

It's clear I'm not going to pee, so I stand up and let my nightgown fall back in place. Terrified of what awaits me, I creep over to the sink, shying away from the mirror. After standing with my gaze aimed down for a minute or two, I summon up the courage and look at myself for the first time since the attack.

My face is so white, I gasp. Even more surprising, I look like I'm twenty-five. All the stress of the house and two kids had started to create some wrinkles around my eyes and mouth, but they're gone. Not even a tiny drop of blood mars the gauzy collar of bandages around my neck. They're as immaculate as when first applied, and my skin isn't even discolored where it peeks past the edge. An icy chill rolls down my back from dread, and I think my heart pumps twice in ten seconds. I raise a shaky hand and grasp the bandage, tugging it down in search of the long, jagged line where the doctors sewed my wound closed. Pristine white skin emerges, without a trace of injury or discoloration.

I keep pulling, tugging, twisting, until the whole bandage tears loose, exposing my neck.

My unblemished, perfect, neck.

"This isn't real. I'm dreaming."

Dumbstruck, my arm falls limp to my side, the bandages dangling from my fingers. Nothing makes any sense. I've always had a fair complexion, but this is ghoulish. My heartbeat is too slow to keep me alive, but I feel fine. I haven't gone to the bathroom in days.

"What's happened to me?" I whisper.

A blemish appears on my cheek in the mirror. I fixate on it, but… it's not a blemish. It's a black tile in the shower behind me. I'm… slightly transparent. My eyes widen and my jaw hangs open. With each passing second, my reflection grows more and more indistinct until it's gone entirely, and I stare at a hollow nightgown.

The bandages slip from my fingers, falling to the carpet by my foot.

Barney keeps singing from the living room.

Anthony and Tammy sing along with the show.

Even the clicking of Danny typing on his laptop sounds like it's coming from the bedroom.

I don't have a reflection.

Shrinking away from the mirror like a little girl frightened of the closet monster, I backpedal until I'm sitting on the edge of the bathtub, staring into space. I'm so shocked, I think I've stopped breathing. That's impossible. I clamp a hand over my mouth and pinch my nose shut, counting to sixty. Once. Twice. Three times. No urge to gasp for air. No lightheadedness.

My hand falls limp into my lap. No desperate rush of air flows into my lungs.

I glance at the mirror, feeling betrayed and abandoned, before staring off into space for a while.

"Well," I deadpan. "This isn't normal."

The End

About the Authors:

J.R. Rain is the international bestselling author of over seventy novels, including his popular Samantha Moon and Jim Knighthorse series. His books are published in five languages in twelve countries, and he has sold more than 3 million copies worldwide.

Please find him at: www.jrrain.com.

~~~~~

Originally from South Amboy NJ, **Matthew S. Cox** has been creating science fiction and fantasy worlds for most of his reasoning life. Since 1996, he has developed the "Divergent Fates" world, in which Division Zero, Virtual Immortality, The Awakened Series, The Harmony Paradox, and the Daughter of Mars series take place.

Matthew is an avid gamer, a recovered WoW addict, Gamemaster for two custom systems, and a fan of anime, British humour, and intellectual science fiction that questions the nature of reality, life, and what happens after it.

He is also fond of cats.

Please find him at www.matthewcoxbooks.com.

Made in the USA
Columbia, SC
10 August 2019